# Stranger Danger

# STRANGER DANGER

### RYAN J. PELTON

Rock House Publishing
*Kansas City*

# *Stranger Danger*

## An Antique Assassin Crime Novel

### Book 2

This is a work of fiction. All of the characters, organizations, locations, and events portrayed in this novel are either product's of the author's imagination or are used fictitiously.

Third Edition

Published by Rock House Publishing
www.rockhousepublishing.com

ISBN 13: 978-1-949420-05-0

# Other Books By Author

**Antique Assassin Crime series**
*Hired Gun (Book 1)*
*Color Blind (Book 3)*
*First Blood (Book 4- prequel)*
**Stand Alone Novels**
*The Boardwalk*
**Shorts**
*Watched*
**The Ricky Rayburn Chronicles**
**Middle Grade Fiction (8-12)**
*Secrets of the Ambassadors*
*Mysterious Pirates of the Pacific (Book 2)*
*Book 3 (2019)*

*"Honor your father and your mother, that your days may be long in the land that the Lord your God is giving you.*
*-Exodus 20:12*

# Chapter 1

The white Ford F-150 sat idle in front of the Leavenworth Prison while her barbed wire gleaned in the late morning sunlight. I played with the radio avoiding the inevitable. My mind raced to former days when dad was home. Days when the family spoke the name George O'Kane without embarrassment.

I killed the engine to the truck, opened the door, adjusted a green John Deere hat, and pinched a wad of tobacco jamming it in my lip.

The prison spanned at least a football field. I peeked at a guard sitting in the tower caressing his gun. He nodded in my direction and I tipped the bill of my hat in response. I heeded the advice of my counselor and gave a little self talk, *it's normal picking up your father in a maximum security prison, on a Tuesday, in January.*

I don't recall ever visiting a penitentiary and its allure formed by *Shawshank Redemption* and the

*Green Mile.* The sea of chain link, barbed wire, and silence didn't make the visit welcoming.

A guard stood behind a solid metal barricaded door with no intention of smiling in my direction. I bent down to peer into a small window, scratched my beard (a go-to nervous twitch), and placed my hand on the beaten-in hat, like a Private saluting a captain in the Army.

I pressed a black button on the intercom. "Beautiful day, ain't it? Is this where I sign in?" I said, mouthing the words to the woman guard.

A stalky black woman, twice my size in weight, slid open a small rectangular window. A steel drawer flapped down and a clip board rested in the middle.

She squawked back, "Please sign and initial on the yellow highlighted marks," speaking through the glass.

The document promised I would not sue if someone stabbed me in the neck with a shiv made of bar soap. I pretended to read the fine print scribbling my name and initials on the proper lines. I glanced up under my hat, smiled, hoping to lighten the mood.

My stomach churned thinking about the impending meeting with an absent father of thirty years.

"If the inmate turns out to be a pain in my neck. Can I bring him back? Is there a 30-day return policy?" I said, sliding the drawer back into the window.

No response.

"Please follow Officer Barnes through the chain link corridor. Do not walk outside the painted arrows on the cement. A second officer will meet you at the end of the corridor and lead you to our offices. You can pick up your inmate there. Questions?"

"What kind of food they serve in here?"

Silence.

I heard a click and the steel door yawned open.

I tipped my cap at the guard, hugged the arrows with my feet, and tried to not step on the heels of the officer leading me down the silent steel corridor.

My heart raced not because of the thousands of people behind bars who could end my life. Nausea because of this day. A day I thought would never happen.

I thought there would be more excitement and less diarrhea.

I didn't even know who to look for. The last blurry picture in my memory was of a dark haired, tall, and strong man pushing me in a swing at Sweeney Park. The last evidence of him before being sent to the pokey.

A guard yelled out in the distance. The sound a muffled blur of noise.

My eyes glued to the painted yellow arrows on

the cement. Each step matched the thumping of my own heart. I peeked up just in time to see the second large steel door with a small window. A guard pushed the door open and waved me in.

"You O'Kane?" A flat-topped guard asked in a deep voice.

"That's the name my mother gave me," I said, with a half-smile.

"Your prisoner is waiting over there," pointing to an office in a large sterile room with a flat screen TV playing CNN on the cement wall.

"They'll check him out and give you his belongings."

"Thank you."

I hesitated, not ready to look toward my father.

I opened the office door and scanned the room. A frail man sat cross-legged on a folding metal chair against the wall. His short grey hair spiked. His blue eyes looked up at me. A large toothy grin emerged on his wrinkled face.

He stuck out both hands.

"Dexter, my son. It's been way too long..."

I didn't recognize him.

The once strong and dark haired man now grey, skinny, and pale.

I gave a soft awkward hug not sure whether to apply the full embrace or resort to the back slap. I chose the latter. I didn't know if my emotions were ready to handle a person I barely knew and relied on family stories for the full dysfunctional mosaic.

A woman wearing a brown prison uniform came out of the corner of the room with a bag full of clothes. "These are his belongings. Please sign here, here, and initial here," handing me a clipboard and placing the bag at my feet.

"Good thing our government doesn't believe in red tape. My hand is cramping up," I said, with a wink.

The woman ignored my humor, gave me an eye, and vanished behind an office desk.

My father ripped the bag from the floor and peered inside. "I haven't seen this junk in almost thirty years. The day they locked me up and threw away the key. This stuff might be worth something," holding up a worn leather wallet, steel lighter, and a brown Members Only jacket.

My father examined the items like a caveman discovering fire.

A guard escorted us out of the office, through the chain link corridor, and to the parking lot. We stood behind a large white steel gate. It opened at the sound of gears needing WD40.

Sunlight poured in.

I stood stiff, shielded my eyes, and waited for the gate to open.

"I'm not sure why I came today. To be honest, I thought you were dead. I'm here. And not sure how to deal with it. This is not a get out of jail free card. You'll find your way in the world outside these walls."

My father held up his hands like freezing in a robbery, "Easy... son. I know things have been weird between us for a long time. But, I want to make things right."

"Long time? Yeah, thirty years is a long time. I was six when you went into this place."

"I was young and stupid. It's not fair you had to grow up without a father. I've learned a lot behind bars."

"Not bad. I had a great dad. Mom remarried after you got locked up. His name is Lester."

These were coping mechanisms for what I felt. That's what my counselor tells me.

"I'm sure he's a great man. I know we can't make up for lost time. But, I'm sure as hell going to try. Can we at least try, son?"

We sauntered over to the truck and jumped inside.

The parking lot was empty.

I stared through the windshield at the white steel gate yawning closed. My father sitting next to me in the passenger seat created a first date awkwardness of the worst kind.

Silence.

A faint rumbling of an engine coming from the rear of the truck peaked my interest. A black car was getting larger in the mirror. It pulled behind us, slammed on the brakes, and an arm came out of the driver window. A rifle shimmered in the sun.

Two shots shattered the back glass of the truck.

I covered my dad like a blanket protecting him from the shower of bullets and glass.

# Chapter 2

The black truck reversed and the sound of squealing tires echoed in the chamber of my ringing ears. Glass covered our bodies as I lay over my father. A jagged piece leaned against my sweaty neck.

I peeked up above the now missing back window and listened for more action.

Nothing.

I whispered in my dad's ear, "You okay?"

No response.

I cleared away a path of broken chards of glass from his neck and placed two fingers over his wrinkled skin.

Heart still beating.

I sat up and glanced out the front of the truck and caught the black vehicle driving at the right side of the parking lot. A debris and dust cloud lifted from behind the speeding vehicle.

I fired up the engine and placed a hand on my father's back. I could feel his skinny ribs moving with bated breath. He moaned, squirmed, and went silent in the passenger seat.

I reached behind the seat in the extended cab and pulled out a black duffel. A Beretta .92FS pistol stared back at me. I yanked on the magazine release button to check ammunition. Full. I laid the black beauty on my lap and gassed the truck.

The truck rumbled and glass danced up and down in the cab. I gave my father a couple looks to check for progress. My truck gained ground on the speeding black vehicle. I placed the gun in my left hand, pulled down my sunglasses with the right, and took aim at the back window of the vehicle.

One. Miss. Two. Miss. Third. Hit.

The vehicle swerved to the left, right, and straight on the two-lane road. I glanced at the rearview mirror to see the prison getting smaller in the distance. A swarm of oak trees hung over the road as our loud vehicles raced down the highway.

I gained on the small pickup truck and hit the brakes as it veered to the left and smashed into a large tree. The front of the radiator spewed water and steam. My truck fishtailed, and I yanked it back to center just past the mangled car. I pulled back around to eye the driver.

The driver kissed the steering wheel and blood rushed down the center of his forehead. I scanned both sides of the road looking for any passersby.

Quiet.

I pressed my face into the arm of my hoodie trying to shield the smell of smoke. The front end of the truck looked like an accordion and fluids squirted from every orifice of the vehicle.

I wiggled the handle of the truck door and reached in for the body. He was still. Blood poured down the middle of his face from a wound in his hairline. The man, dark-skinned, brown hair, and wearing a yellow hoodie. Not much older than twenty-five.

The truck smoked and sizzled from the engine compartment and out of the dashboard.

I wrapped my arms under his armpits, drug the body around the passenger side of the vehicle, and laid him on a soft patch of grass and leaves near a ditch. I stood over the body for a moment to get a better look. No match in my brain.

I checked both sides of the road, sprinted back to my truck, and set my Beretta on the center console. I grabbed the gun and poked my father. "You alive?"

He was now making noise and moaning, awakening from his short sleep. "I thought two people would die today."

My father moaned, and his eyes fluttered, as I sped past the burning vehicle. I watched the truck in the rearview ignite in flames as we fled.

My father fluttered his eyes and raised his head from his short sleep. He looked down at the tags of glass clinging to his Member's Only jacket. "What happened? You okay, son?" he said, looking me over.

"Everything's fine now. We had a situation after the prison visit."

My father scanned the surrounding wooded road from the passenger window and picked glass from his bloody arm. "Did everything go okay at the prison? Did they harass you?"

"Not exactly. But, not a good day for the man in the yellow hoodie."

"Who? Is he a guard?"

I placed my hand on my father's leg picking out a shard of glass. "It doesn't matter. Why don't you take a nap? We have a long ride to LeClaire."

"Where's LeClaire?"

I pressed the gas, and the truck worked hard down the Kansas highway. "It's in Missouri. My home. Maybe your home, depending on how you behave," I said, with a grin.

# Chapter 3

The F-150 hummed along highway seventy with a whistling sound coming through the shot out back window. I squinted at the sun in full view over Missouri on this January day.

Most of the three hour ride home to LeClaire spent in silence. I didn't know what to say to a man who I'd only known thirty years ago. My father broke the silence. "Who's the President?" he asked, playing with a LeClaire Gazette newspaper on the floorboards.

I raised an eyebrow in his direction. "Really? You didn't have newspapers or a TV in prison?" I asked.

"We did. I didn't care all that much. You lose time, and the belief for the existence of an outside world."

"You went through a bunch of Presidents in thirty years. Reagan, Bush #1, Clinton, Bush #2, and now, Obama."

"Is that the black fella?"

I rolled my eyes, "Yes, the first African American President. Is this a problem?"

"Not for me. But your grandfather is turning over in his grave with a black President. Let's say small town Missouri was not open minded in his era."

"It's still not the hope for a progressive America," I said, with a wink.

"A lot of guys in the joint don't like Obama. Didn't do enough for minority communities."

I shook my head in agreement, not having a strong opinion, being a white man from Irish descent living in LeClaire Missouri.

"How are the Royals doing? I miss my baseball," he said, flipping to the sports page in the paper.

I reached into my wallet, and held up a ticket stub, "Made it to the World Series last year. Lost to the San Francisco Giants. Bumgarner pitched out of his mind. I went to Game 1."

He lit up, scanned the ticket, and slapped his knee. "That's wonderful. The Royals won the World Series the year I got locked up. They must have been a good team for a lot of years."

"Not so much. The last time they made it to the World Series was thirty years ago."

He frowned, handed back the ticket. "Oh."

"How'd you become a Royals fan?"

"I used to listen to games with your grandfather on the radio every Sunday night. That was before TV had a million channels, old school. One of my big regrets," he said, turning to stare out on the highway.

"Regret?" I asked.

"I wanted to share my love of baseball with my son. That never happened."

I didn't respond.

"I'm excited to meet the family. Have you mentioned me? Tell them I'm coming?"

I ignored the question and stared out the window. Embarrassed by my incarcerated biological father and still didn't know what to think of it all. "I might've mentioned you a time or two."

"Kids?" he asked.

"Twin boys. Eighteen months. I hope you know this makes things complicated for my family."

My father rummaged through the brown bag of belongings sitting on the floor and lit up a cigarette. He rolled down the truck window and blew out the smoke. "Cigarettes sure don't keep after thirty years," he said, spewing out smoke, coughing, and staring at the limp cancer stick flopping in the wind.

Smirked at the smoking catastrophe and put a wad of chewing tobacco in my lip, "I see we have some of the same bad habits."

"No special accommodations for me, Dex. I screwed things up. Don't want to make things weird with you or grandchildren," he said.

"You don't get the right to be family right now. You walked away. Today, you are a family friend.

I'm helping you out until you get on your feet," I said, waving smoke out of my eyes.

My father stared down at the floor and then looked up, "Whatever you want, son. Where'd you meet your wife?"

Reached down and turned off the radio. I ripped the limp cigarette hanging off his lip. Flicked it out my window.

"I need to tell you something," I said, with force.

"Anything son, what is it?"

"A couple years ago my first wife..." I paused and tried to form words, "... died, along with our son. Killed in a car accident. I met Samantha in a bar when I was trying to get my life back together. We got married, and she got pregnant six months later. This is my family now."

My father reached out his calloused hand and placed it on my leg. "Oh, son. I had no idea."

"Yeah it was a shitty time. I lost my mind, became a drunk, and almost lost my business. Still trying to work through some stuff."

"I can't imagine. What kind of business do you have?"

"I'm an antique dealer."

"Huh, that sounds like interesting work."

"It's interesting when we're making money. My business partner is my best friend John Wood. Samantha does the books. It's kind of a family business."

"Good to hear you're doing well Dexter. I'm

sorry about your first wife and kid. That must be the hardest thing you've ever gone through."

I smiled, "Yep, until today, when you meet your incarcerated father after thirty years."

"That's deserved."

I locked eyes on an eagle flying over the highway as the sun settled in the Missouri sky. "I know this might sound like a strange question. Why did you go to prison? Mom never told me."

Dad got silent. He pulled out another cigarette and dangled it in his lip without lighting it. He breathed in and sighed.

"Yeah, that."

"We've got time. One more hour to LeClaire," I said, watching a blue mileage sign flash by the truck window.

"Thirty years ago... I got in over my head with a gambling ring. Some guys from work, were making a fortune betting on the T-Bones, our minor league baseball team. I got in over my head, lost my shirt, pants, shoes, and couldn't pay back my bookies."

"How much over your head?"

"Let's say... my bookies either wanted cash or would take it in blood."

My eyes were alive and interest piqued listening to the story, "What did you do?"

"I robbed First National Bank of LeClaire. And... I shot a security guard trying to get away."

I shook my head trying to absorb the informa-tion. "Holy crap. You're a thief and a murderer. I knew you were a dirt bag, but this is not what I gathered from family stories."

"Thanks for the compliment. I'm thankful the judge was lenient and only gave me thirty years. This was my first offense."

"Can I ask you a question?"

"I have nothing to hide."

"You remember the attack at the prison?"

"I remember a loud BANG. Something about a man in a hoodie..."

"A truck pulled up and fired on us. You blacked out, and the driver crashed into a tree while speeding away."

My father paused for a beat. "People might look for me. Some terrible people."

"The guy in the black car?" I asked.

"Maybe. My bookies were part of a family business in LeClaire. From what I gathered in prison there are men who still want payment from thirty years ago. I don't know who the hoodie guy might be, but probably connected to this family."

"No way. You think these guys still want money? These bookies are probably all dead. They must think you're dead. Like I did," I said, with a wink.

"There's one little detail I didn't mention. The man I killed in the bank was a brother of the family. They want more than my debts, they want my head."

"It sounds like you messed with the wrong family."

"I did. And I'm only making things more complicated for you, and your family. Drop me off at a hotel and I'll figure something out."

The truck slowed as we veered off the highway. A couple turns and I sped down a gravel road. I pulled into my driveway.

Leaned over to my father and spoke in a soft tone. "Not sure what kind of shit storm you're swimming in. Don't know why I'm doing this... but, you can stay with us for the night. If my family gets into any kind of danger you're out. We'll find accommodations for you tomorrow. There's a nice Holiday Inn Express in town," I said.

"Thanks son," he said, leaning in for a hug.

I pulled back and opened the truck door.

"We're here. And I already hugged you once today."

# Chapter 4

The wooden steps creaked as we climbed to the landing. I bear-hugged the brown bag of the only possessions my father had on earth, and the clothes on his back. My lungs stung from the brisk winter air. Our newer ranch style home was still littered with Christmas lights. I rattled my keys, pushed open a red door, and a large pine wreath chimed from hanging silver bells.

The holiday season was good to Antique Adventures affording me nice gifts for a change. The business almost failed a few short years earlier after Lisa and Spencer's death. Now, new wife, twin eighteen month boys, step daughter, things are looking up.

My father flicked the pine needles, "Nice wreath. Haven't seen one of these in thirty years. Leavenworth didn't believe in decorating. Fear of stringing up the guards with twinkle lights in a jail riot," he said, with a grin.

I gave a half smile and pretended to be okay with

the situation. Bringing home dad from prison didn't feel as comfortable as I thought. It felt more like bringing home my first child and being filled with fear and anxiety.

I yelled for Samantha.

No answer.

"That's weird. Wonder where my family is." I said, throwing my green John Deere hat on the dining room table.

"Can't wait to meet them," my dad said, pacing the living room examining photographs on the wall.

I walked over to my father as he leaned into a frame of my family at the beach last summer. Jammed a hand into his shoulder. He leaned to one side and stared up at me with a crooked smile.

"Before you get too comfortable. Let's get this straight. You're just a picker friend I'm helping out. That's our story for now. Got it?"

"I'm not sure if this is cool kid lingo. But, if you don't mind me asking, what is a picker?"

"I told you. I'm an antique collector. That's how I support my family."

"Picker... like a trash collector? Boogers? What?"

I reached up to a bookcase and pulled down a silver candle stick. "How much you think this is worth?" handing it to my father.

He lifted the candlestick up and down pretending to inspect it like a collector on Antique Road Show. "I don't know. Thirty bucks."

I chuckled and snatched it back out of his hands. "This baby is worth three thousand bucks. I found it on a pick in the back woods of Carthage, Missouri. It's from 1700s England."

"So what does this have to do with picking... or whatever you call it?"

"You may recall from the drive up here. I own a business called Antique Adventures with my partner John. I travel the back roads, highways, and byways of America looking for rusty gold. We find rare items of history, antiques to the laymen, and sell em' in our shop. We like to think of ourselves as antique archeologists. You need the facts to keep our stories straight," I said, placing the candle stick on the table.

"You pay the bills with this trash... I mean rare items of history?"

I waved my hands around the room. "You see this house. I paid cash for it last year with my trash collecting. Not bad for a dumpster diver, huh?"

My father shook his head up and down. "Not bad. You must get your business savvy from your old man."

"Ha. Everything is earned. I work long and hard, to provide for my family, and make our business go. Not giving you credit for some business gene."

"I used to buy and sell things."

"What, drugs?"

"Nooo. I used to buy old cars and fix them up

for money. That's how I paid for your diapers. I got good."

I didn't want to acknowledge that maybe my business savvy and love for collecting things might have come from this jail-bird. "That's nice. But it sounds like your business acumen failed you. A lot of savvy businessmen do time in prison," I said, slapping his frail back.

My father glided over to a brown leather couch, reached for a pillow, and held it against his chest. He waved me over. "Yeah about that. I need to tell you something, Dexter."

I pulled out a chair from the dining room table, placed it in from of him, and kept an eye on the door waiting for the family to return. "Make it brief before my family comes home. We need to keep our stories straight."

"The man who shot at us today might look for money. A lot of money."

"I know, you already told me. No one will make you pay a debt from over thirty years ago. Most people assume you're dead. Including myself..." I said, with a wink.

He placed the pillow to his right, put his head between his legs, and then looked up wide eyed. "I didn't give you all the details. A guy in prison said the juice is still running from my gambling debts. They want their money plus interest."

"How do you know this dude in prison is a reliable source?"

"He is, trust me."

"How much juice you talking?" I said, pulling out my wallet.

"Put away your wallet son. You'll need more than what you got in there. My life is not even worth these debts."

"It can't be that much. You went to prison thirty years ago."

"Half a million."

I shot up from the chair, picked up my stress-reliever-ball from the end table and squeezed. "Shit dad. You get outta prison, owe half-a-mil, and we almost get our heads blown off. This is not what I had in mind for a family reunion."

He choked up with tears. "This is why your mother gave up on me after I got locked up. I was always getting our family into trouble with stupid ideas. She was fed up... son, your father is such a failure."

I set the ball down, plopped on the couch, and put an arm around his shoulders. "Don't think I'm happy about this. I was already hesitant when I got the call from prison. This is not a get out of jail-free-card. Knowing what I know, now, makes things complicated. But, we'll figure something out. That's what O'Kane's do. I know some people."

He smirked, tears dripping on the brown carpet. "Who do you know? Trash collecting buddies who specialize in helping ex-cons."

"Let's say I know people who handle these kinds of situations."

The front door swung open and a woman's voice called my name. It was Samantha.

# Chapter 5

The cool breeze of January blasted into the front room. A blonde haired woman wearing yoga pants, puffy vest, Nike hat, and running shoes, burst through the door.

"Dexter, can you help with the boys?" Samantha asked, as two toddlers, with matching snow jackets waddled into the house. A young blonde girl danced in behind them.

Bent down on both knees I held out my arms as the two small creatures leapt. Kissed the blue-eyed boys on the cheek as they giggled.

I messed up their hair. "Were you guys good for your momma? No tantrums?" I asked with a smile.

The twin boys nodded.

I turned to the girl. "How 'bout you?"

She stuck out a hip and gave a crooked smile. "You know I'm a princess, Dexter."

My wife, boys, and step-daughter are gifts from God. They came when dealing with the loss of my first family. There's not a day when I look down into their cribs and bedrooms and do not thank God for them. Not always with the same amount of gratitude when they are crying and throwing tantrums through the night. But, no amount of crying can change my love for them.

I set the boys down and rose to look my sexy wife up and down. "You seem underdressed for January."

"I took the kid's to the YMCA. I did yoga."

"Trying to keep up with your husband?" I asked, flexing a bicep.

"Do you even know where the gym is?"

"I stay in shape other ways."

"Chasing John around bars and pizza parlors?"

"No way. I lift antiques into the truck every day. That's how I got these biceps, hon."

Samantha set down a bag of groceries on the dining room table and burrowed her eyebrows. "Make your biceps useful and take these to the kitchen, He-Man."

She turned toward my father standing awkwardly in the middle of the room. "Who's this?"

Lisa blurted out in typical kid fashion, "He's old."

I shook my head and gave her a look of 'get in your room' with piercing eyes. My father floated across the room before I could say another word and stuck out his wrinkled hands. "Name is Frank. A friend of your husband. We are old picker buddies," he said, winking in my direction.

I chimed in, cutting him off, for fear of screwing up our scheme of silence. I wasn't ready to tell Samantha the true back story. "Yeah. We used to pick together in Western Missouri, at the Miller's place."

Samantha nodded, looking my dad up and down, with a puzzled look. "Okay..."

The Miller place is one of my favorite picking spots. A large twenty acre plot with enough barns and storage units to fund my business for a year. I once found a 1923 Indian Motorcycle and sold to a collector for thirty grand.

Samantha wiped her hand on the side of her yoga pants, and stuck it out, "The Miller Farm is one of my favorite picking spots. Every time Dex goes, I know the kid's will have new shoes... or a pair for momma," she said, blowing me a fake kiss.

I felt nausea coming amidst the web of lies swirling around the living room. I tried to cut them off before they intertwined and twisted like Highway 24 after a deer smeared by an eighteen wheeler.

"So, Frank will stay with us for a few days. He's not from LeClaire and needs to get settled. He lived in Kansas for the last thirty years."

"I thought you were picking buddies?" Samantha asked.

"Yeah... we are. Frank used to come up to Missouri for better picking. And, to get away from some family issues."

Sweat formed under my armpits. The web of lies mounting. I was certain Samantha knew we were trying to pull a fast one on her.

"Family can be tough. Did Dexter tell you about Uncle Pete?" she asked.

Uncle Pete's my dad's brother he doesn't know is alive, yet. When dad went to prison everyone bailed on him. Even Pete, his only living brother.

My father put his head down and cracked a small smile. "That's funny. I used to have a brother named Pete. He was the best."

"What happened to him?" I asked pretending not to know.

"Oh, he died. I got a note in prison..."

Samantha blurted out, "Prison?"

My dad stumbled over his words, "Silly me. I didn't mean prison. Sometimes family feels like prison. I meant to say, Kansas, in the mail, while in Kansas."

"I'm sorry to hear Frank. Well, we'll be your family for the next few days," Samantha said, with a dimpled smile.

I turned to the front plate glass window and heard a loud rev of an engine. Samantha and my dad small talked in the background. I ducked to see what's going on in the front of the house. A black Toyota 4×4 pulled into the driveway.

Crash.

A brick shattered through the window and glass covered the floor missing the children in their bouncy seats by inches. In reaction, Frank pulled Samantha to the floor to protect her from the glass.

I ran to the front door almost ripping the door off its hinges. I stared at the red taillights of the truck speeding down the quiet country road.

"Is there something you need to tell me Dexter?" Samantha asked, from the fetal position on the floor, dad's arm wrapped around her strong body.

# Chapter 6

I knelt down, examined a red brick laying in a sea of shattered glass. Brushed off the shards and read a message scribbled in black ink. Presence of my wife, dad, and crying children breathing on my neck. I read message aloud:

Georgie boy... We need our money!

Samantha ruffled her nose in confusion, ripped the brick from my hands, and mouthed the words, "Who's Georgie boy?"

The collision of lies was sitting on the end of my tongue and swirling in my brain. I didn't want to lie to Samantha. The homecoming of my father needed discussion. But I wasn't ready; scared, and unsure of how an absent relationship of thirty years with my father could be repaired. My relationship with Samantha began with a lie, when I didn't have the guts to tell her my wife and kid died in a car accident. It sickened me I never discussed my dad, at least not in honesty.

My father shot up from the leather couch, raised

his hand proving guilt, and snatched the brick from Samantha's hand. "I'm Georgie Boy. My mother changed my name after emigrating from Ireland. She said it was easier to pronounce and more Irish sounding," George said, flipping the brick over in his hand.

The red brick lay flat in his large calloused hand. He turned it over a couple more times, like a cook flipping pizza dough, and commented on the bad penmanship. A trickle of sweat fell from his temple.

Samantha stood with arms akimbo and scanned the suspicious room, "Dexter, honey. Why is Frank's name now Georgie boy? What's going on?" Samantha asked.

I stammered trying to devise a plan that made sense. The babies kept howling in the background while Samantha jammed two pacifiers in their mouths. The noise added to the challenge of devising a plausible explanation.

"People change their names all the time. George is Frank, Frank is George, tomato, t-o-m-a-t-o, who cares," I said, with my hands jammed under my armpits as they pooled with sweat.

"Are you telling me everything? You seem nervous," Samantha asked.

"It just feels a little hot in here. Anyone else hot?" I asked wiping my face.

"No honey, it's January," Samantha said.

I wasn't ready to spill the beans about my dad

and needed time to get out of this mess. I blurted first thought came to mind, "Georgie Boy is not an old picking buddy," I said, hanging my head, "he's my lover, I'm into older man," I said, not able to hold back a laugh.

Samantha rocked one of our children, gave me a stern look, and punched me with her free arm. "Stop playing games. No dudes would ever go for you," she said, giving me a wink, "what is going on here?"

George placed the brick on an end table and crossed his arms. A bead of sweat bubbled up on his wrinkled and age spotted head.

I nodded at George for permission to spill the beans. I was done trying to navigate a trail of lies.

"I'm not Dexter's old friend... or lover..." he paused wiping the sweat, "I'm Dexter's father."

The room went silent.

Sounds of suckling children on pacifiers. A truck rumbled up the street in the distance. My heart beat fast.

I removed our son Josiah from my wife's arms, with hopes of protection, if she lost her lid. "I didn't want to tell you about my father, yet. This is all new for me, and us. I wasn't sure if letting George back into my life was a good idea. A kind of trial run," I said, waiting for a positive response.

"I thought your dad died?" Samantha asked.

I smiled, gave Josiah a slow rock, and adjusted the pacifier as he began to squeal. I could feel my dad staring through me. Waiting to hear my answer.

"Yeah, about that. It's the standard answer in the O'Kane family when asked about Dad," glancing at my dad, "He spent the last thirty years in jail. We thought he would die there, who knew?" I said, hoping Samantha would laugh with me. Not so much.

My father raised both hands in the air, "Surprise! I'm alive," shaking his head in disgust, "You tell people I died?"

I nodded in agreement.

"Jail? Your dad is a frigging criminal?" Samantha said, placing her hands on the top of her blonde hair like she was fighting a migraine.

George smiled at Samantha trying to diffuse the situation. "Prison wasn't so bad. Three squares a day, cable, and it gives you time to think. It made me a better person. I'm no threat to you or society anymore."

I walked over to the end table and picked up the brick. Tossed it a couple times. "Now that the cat is out of the bag and before the family reunion goes any further. I have a question. Why in the hell are bricks shattering my window and almost killing my children? If you are no threat to society, explain this one, Georgie boy."

I had hoped the diversion question would diffuse the rage Samantha exuded in the corner of the room. Waited for my dad to answer, trying not to make eye contact with her.

George sunk into the back of the couch, hands in jacket pockets, and crossed his legs.

"We should talk about the brick."

# Chapter 7

We sat around the living room like a dysfunctional family having an intervention for a drunk uncle. I couldn't believe the nightmare my father was becoming. Not sure if the shooting at the prison related to his shenanigans. And now the brick in the window. This was not the homecoming I imagined in my head.

I spoke first, "Let's talk about the brick. Tell me why you're no harm to my family and society?"

My father's drooping eyes told the story. He stared down at his generic tennis shoes and popped back up. "As I told you before, I got caught up in a gambling ring thirty years ago. The Buffone's were an influential Italian family in LeClaire and used to run things. These two brother's ran a bookkeeping gig for making bets on local sports and other events. They were the go-to guys for any gambling in LeClaire. If you know what I mean."

The tick of a clock drowning out attention on my father. I regretted bringing him back into my life. Didn't care about his safety. Wanted him gone. I focused back into the story, "So why does a bookie from thirty years ago still want your gambling debts? This doesn't make sense," I said, glancing over to my wife sitting in a chair.

Samantha ignored my look.

George became agitated sitting on our brown leather sofa. He wiped his sweaty palms on his Khakis, "There's more to the story. A lot more" he said, grasping his hands together and trying to formulate coherent words.

I waved him to continue.

"I met an Italian guy in prison named Joe. He's connected to the Buffone family, and knew I owed money. To pay off my debts he helped me run a side business from inside the joint. I used past connections in LeClaire to pay the bookies. It worked well until..."

My father paused, took a deep breath, and shook his head not looking me in the eye. A tear slid down the side of his wrinkled skin.

"Until what? You said it worked well... until... what?" I asked.

"The business worked well until someone got killed."

Tears were now streaming down his face soaking the legs of his pants. He convulsed in a crumpled ball on the couch.

"Who got killed?" I asked.

My father raised his red and tear soaked face sniffling for words, "Your mother."

I shot up from the couch, and paced around the room, with hands on my head. I tossed my John Deere hat across the room, "Wait a minute. Mom got killed over your gambling debts. That's not possible. She died of a heart attack years ago."

George placed his hands over his face and tried to talk through sobs and mumbling, "The side business failed. People were not paying and my connections dried up. The Buffone brothers told me if I didn't pay someone would die. It got personal. They murdered your mother."

The room spun, and I didn't know what to think or feel. I hated my dad and couldn't believe I ever picked up the phone when the prison called for his release.

I replayed in my mind ten years ago the phone call from the police. My mother died at home. Heart attack. I knew she was in bad health and her ticker would take her down. I thought nothing of it.

"So, Mom didn't die of a heart attack?"

"No. The Police Chief in LeClaire at the time owed me a favor. He covered up the murder and made the call on my behalf. The entire town had no clue. Our family had no clue."

I went numb. The thought of my mother being murdered by a bunch of sweaty Italians made me nauseous. I wanted to hurt my father and find this family.

I switched to an analytical mindset and tried to keep my emotions at bay. I tried to pretend that my father's story was all a lie and anytime now Ashton Kutcher would walk in and tell me we got punk'd.

"Let me recap. You owe money to an Italian mob family. Work a deal in prison that goes bad. Mom gets murdered. And now people are throwing bricks through my window because these thirty-year-old debts need payment from your ass. Sound right?"

My dad sat in silence only to nod in agreement.

"I'm sorry, son. I had no intention of bringing you into this mess. I've caused enough trouble to the family. Please forgive me."

I ignored his plea for grace and got back to business, "How much do you owe?"

George stumbled to get the words out, "A million."

"What? You told me half-a-mill earlier today."

"Half-a-mill didn't sound as bad in my head. Thirty years is a long time. Interest adds up, I guess."

Samantha left the room and slammed the door of the bedroom. The twins cried.

# Chapter 8

The rocking chair moved in time with the warm Missouri winds. At least warm for January. My makeshift window of cardboard, duct tape, and elbow grease fluttered in the wind behind my head. The red glowing tip of a new cigar gave a little light to the porch.

It was 3 AM.

I tried talking with Samantha after she stormed out of the living room earlier in the evening. She wanted nothing to do with me. Tired of the lies. I don't blame her. I didn't want to see me either.

My father slept on the couch in a pair of my old sweatpants and yellow Antique Adventures tee shirt. A slogan pasted on the front, "One man's junk. Another man's treasure," with a rusty Indian Motorcycle leaning against a tree.

We all needed a new start in the morning. The rat's nest of lies and gambling debts made sleep not an option. I rocked back and forth in the chair scanning the sleeping town of LeClaire.

Flickers of light popping in the night's sky. A person waking to work the early shift at the electrical plant. The reds of taillights from a long night at the bar. This was the town where I began. The place my father used to push me in a swing only miles from this rocking chair. I hoped to revisit those days in a idealistic way. Not as a child. But, as a man who grew up without his biological father. I hoped for my kids to know their grandfather.

I tapped the side of a glass bowl watching the ashes of my cigar float into the bottom. The red glow of my cancer stick the only light on our quiet road.

Light grew in the distance from my neighbor's farm. Beginning of life in the impending sunrise. I imagined Mr. Branson firing up the tractor and putting in a full day's work.

Farming is tough business in LeClaire and not what it once was. The economic dip, rising gas prices, housing development, and large corporations ignoring the little guys. Mr. Branson is scraping by.

I say a short prayer asking God to provide all his needs today.

I couldn't complain. Even if the return of my father, who I didn't know was alive months earlier, is turning out to be a pain in my side... life is good. The shop continues to make money, good money, even in a slow economy. People buy stuff to ease the pain of life regardless of what the economic analysts tell you. My new wife, older daughter, and the twins, are keeping me sane after losing Lisa and Spencer. Not replacements, but gifts, a new start for me. I thank God for them every day.

I yanked the cigar from my dry mouth and examined the tip which ceased burning red. Dad wouldn't escape the reservoirs of my mind. He weighed on me.

I felt a responsibility as the son. I remember learning in Sunday School, as a kid, about "honoring your parents" from the Bible. It didn't make sense to me when I was six, but it does now. My father is older and been in prison for thirty years. I can't imagine what happened inside the "joint" and the things he saw.

I wanted to help him. But, didn't. I wanted him around. But, didn't. The return of the Prodigal Dad was confusing.

I leaned back in the rocker and stared out into the distance. I relit the stogie, puffed hard, trying to restart the dead tip. I imagined if I sucked hard enough I'd enter another time continuum where dads didn't go to prison and loved their families until the end. It didn't work. I was still here. Dad was still sleeping. Debts still loomed. The creaking of wood under my feet reminded me that life is never perfect. It is flexible and all over.

My eyes got heavy.

The rocking motion of the chair lulled me to sleep. I felt the cigar slip out of my mouth and was about to fall on my lap. I awoke, extinguished the cigar in the glass bowl, and snuck back into the house to catch a couple hours of sleep before work.

Maybe all of this was a bad dream.

# Chapter 9

I stumbled awake to a knock on the front door. Glanced down realizing my only protection between the door and the world were boxer briefs and a 2005 LeClaire rodeo tee shirt. Wiped my eyes and crotch to see who came for a visit.

I nudged the door open to see two men standing on the porch with LeClaire PD identification plastered on their shirt pockets. A black police cruiser shot sparkles of light from the morning sun off its pristine paint.

I figured a passerby must have called the police after the brick incident. Al Mulder lived five acres to the left. Old man, dogs, and unofficial crime prevention liaison for the county. The rumor is he failed the Police Academy, and being the local snitch, keeps him in the game.

A large flat top, wide shoulders, and gut hanging over a black leather belt with gold emblem came into view. A smaller, nimble, and fit young officer, not more than twenty-five, stood to his right.

"What brings LeClaire's finest to my house this morning? Even before my morning coffee," I said, trying to cover my man parts behind the door.

The flat top peeked at the other officer and gave him a raised eyebrow. He stood stiff, gripped his belt with both hands and gave it a wiggle, and spoke, "I'm Officer Brown and this is Metcalf. We got a call about a disturbance on your property."

The smaller officer peered over my shoulder and investigated the makeshift cardboard window. It pulsated in and out from the morning breeze. I tried to downplay the situation, "No big deal. We got a brick through the window last night. Probably just kids from the local high school looking for something to do on a Friday night. Not much to do in LeClaire, am I right?" I said, slapping the flat-topped officer in the arm, realizing the clothes situation I jumped back behind the door.

He examined his muscular arm as if a fly had landed and flew off. The smaller officer pulled out a small black writing pad and flipped to the first page, "Any details you can give about these kids to help our investigation?" he asked, ready with pen in hand.

I sneered, "Investigation? I don't think a couple kids having a little fun on a Friday night is worth an investigation and precious taxpayer dollars. My insurance will cover it," I said, with a grin.

"Can I have your name, sir?" flat top asked.

"Dexter O'Kane."

The officer folded his hands and spoke in a softer tone, "Mr. O'Kane. We take law enforcement and protecting the people of LeClaire very serious. Damages were done to your property and we don't want this to happen again. Even if this was a bunch of kids screwing around on a Friday night. What details can you give us? Did you see a vehicle or any suspicious people around before the incident?"

I crossed my arms and laughed on the inside thinking about the serious speech about protecting the people of LeClaire. I don't think these guys see much action living in a small town. This was their Super Bowl.

I itched my armpit and scanned the yard behind the officers. I tried to come up with a convincing story so I could get coffee, "My family and I were having dinner. We heard a large crash in the living room after the brick broke through the window. I ran out to find a car racing north down the street. I couldn't identify color, make, model, or any people inside the car. Just red taillights in the distance, it was dark," I said.

The smaller officer scribbled notes at a ferocious pace glancing up and down with my every word, "Any reason someone would want to harm your family? Do you have enemies in LeClaire?"

I snickered and tapped the inside of the door post, "Enemies? I'm a small business owner, born and raised in LeClaire, and love this town like my own children. The only enemies are the IRS who keep taking all my money and the Kansas City Chiefs who break my heart every football season. Other than these two. No. No enemies."

Both men smiled in unison looking at one another, "We love this town too. That's why we need to do our due diligence, sir," the smaller officer said.

"Would you have the brick that broke your window?" flat top said, as he poked my cardboard fix-job with a finger.

My stomach churned thinking about the message on the brick. I didn't want to enter another round of lies and needed to think fast, "Uh, did I say brick? I meant a bb-gun, maybe a rock. I don't know. Everything happened so fast," I said, trying to not look the officers in the eyes.

The smaller officer raised an eyebrow and kept scribbling on the notepad. "Is your family okay? Anyone hurt from the broken window?"

I placed my hands to my side remembering, I didn't have any pants on, "They're fine. Other than normal family drama, am I right?" I asked, looking for a high five that never came. The smaller officer gave me a puzzled glance and kept writing his notes.

The smaller officer said, "I know all about the drama. Twin girls at home. Enough estrogen to make a man want to cry," he said, not looking up from the pad.

I nodded in agreement. "Funny. I have twin boys. Maybe we should arrange their marriages."

We all laughed.

"That should be enough for now, Mr. O'Kane. Thanks for the time. If you need anything, please call the department. LPD is here to serve you," said flat top, with a salute.

I fought back laughter and saluted the officer. I now felt the cold punching me in the gut and realized again... no pants. The cruiser drove off into the distance kicking up road dust.

I bent over and placed two hands on my thighs and sighed in relief. My father opened the screen door and peeked around the corner to catch my attention.

He whispered, "Was that the police?"

I held up my hand, "Don't worry. They don't know a thing."

# Chapter 10

The January sun warmed our faces as we sipped coffee and made casual conversation. I glanced at dad on the porch day dreaming of what I envisioned normal kids did with their non-incarcerated fathers. A son, his dad, eating popsicles, playing catch, talking about life and grown up stuff. But, that was never the case with my "real" dad. Those popsicles shared with Lester my stepdad. Good man, just not my dad. I always had the sense that our relationship was incomplete.

I came back to earth.

Dad set an Antique Adventures mug on a wooden side table on the porch, "Why were the cops here? You didn't turn me in did ya?" he said, nervously bouncing his frail knees up and down.

I shook my head denying the accusation. "Neighbor must of called after commotion of the broken window. He's kind of the unofficial citizen on patrol. Who knows? I took care of it," I said, dipping my face into the mouth of a large coffee cup.

My father's face became tender like he wanted to say something but couldn't find the words, "What did you tell them?" he asked.

"Teenagers looking for fun on a Friday night. There's not much to do after the basketball game is over."

My dad almost spit out his coffee and agreed with a nod, "In high school, after the basketball game, we'd cruise up and down Main Street picking up girls. We would meet up at Freddy's. Best burger in LeClaire. That's where I met your mother," he said, face lighting up.

Eyes wide, I gave him a slap on his skinny frail leg, "You dog... cruising for girls on a Friday night. Please tell me more. Mom must've been desperate for love," I said.

My dad rubbed his calloused hands together focused on speech like recalling the details of walking on the moon, "I remember it like yesterday. A Friday night after a basketball game the usual suspects, what we called our group, Johnny, Manny, and Billy, were cruising looking for girls to eat with, and then make out. In that order. We pulled into Freddy's and there sat your mother. She was a cheerleader and lounged across the diner in a red booth, smiling, laughing, and her blonde hair up in a beehive. It was almost loved at first sight."

I hit my dad in the arm, "You dog. Did you kiss her?" I said, realizing that was a disgusting thing to think about.

He lowered his head as if he'd just received the worst news ever, "Not that night. I tried to give her a line and spilled a milkshake all over her red cheerleading skirt. Her friends called me milkshake for the next year. The making out came later. I was never that good with the girls," he said, tears now dripping onto the dusty porch floor, "I would do anything for your mother. Loved her more than my own life."

Right on cue, tears filled my face, as I thought about Lisa, Spencer, and the love we shared. I knew exactly what my father was feeling, "You know what dad? Our stories are the same. I met my first wife, Lisa, at a basketball game. She was a cheerleader too. Funny how life can be," I said, staring off into the yard.

Dad reached for the last sips of coffee and made a sigh, "I know you don't want advice from your old man. I have no right to give it. But, when you find a good woman, you hang onto her. No matter the cost. You hear?" he said, with puffy red eyes.

We both nodded, and I changed the subject, "Well, enough girl talk. We need to talk about our situation. Figure things out," I said, wiping tear residue from my cheek.

"Good, son. I've been thinking about it too. It's best I leave and figure things out on my own. Probably just move away and find a quiet place to land. I don't want to cause harm to your family," he said.

I listened and thought the offer made sense considering the circumstance. But, something in me was resistant, hesitant, holding me back. I didn't like an old man fending for himself against a Mob family. I knew my dad abandoned the family years ago but the thought of him getting hurt sickened me. The "honor your parents" thing haunted my soul, "Don't you think these guys will find you, and kill you, if you don't pay?" I said, standing to my feet, and pacing up and down the front porch.

My father stared at me and gave me a confused look with my response. I don't think he expected it, "I don't know. The thought of putting you, Samantha, and the twins in danger, is not worth it. I already screwed up my family thirty years ago and don't want to do it again," he said, tears returning.

I leaned against the wooden posts of the front porch and stared off across the yard to a group of oak trees tipping in the breeze, "Dad, there's something I need to tell you."

He ignored my comment, "You've done enough son. The fact you picked me up in prison after thirty years makes me indebted for life. You didn't have to do it, I wouldn't. But, you did. I'm just glad we could spend a few hours together and I could meet your beautiful family. I'm proud of you son. But, it's time I go."

I glided across the squeaky wooden porch and

stood over him, "Dad, you didn't hear me. There's something I need to tell you. Come with me," I said, nodding toward the back of the house.

He glanced up, tears in his face, and raised an interested eyebrow, "Okay, son."

# Chapter 11

We stood in front of a weathered red barn. It had AA (Antique Adventures) tattooed on the doors. I fiddled with a black padlock and slid the doors open. The aged barn, with white trim, stationed in the back of the house used for cows, horses, and other livestock by the previous owner.

Now it had other purposes.

"What is this place?" my dad asked, scanning the vaulted wooden rafters.

The left side of the barn housed a large handcrafted L-shaped table covered with vials, beakers, chemicals, and glass mixing containers. In the middle, against the far wall, a rack of rifles, handguns, and bulletproof vests hung from a variety of hooks. The right side, outfitted with two forty inch computer monitors, LCD flat screen TV, photographs of people pinned to the wall, and a rectangular whiteboard with notes scribbled across the front.

I opened my arms wide across my chest and twirled around the room, "This is what I wanted to show you. I told you earlier I knew people who helped in sticky situations. I'm those people," I said, with a half grin.

"I thought you were a junk collector? I mean, antique dealer. Isn't that what the AA initials are on the front of the barn," my father asked.

I smiled and tried to articulate exactly what I did on the side, "The initials are a diversion. I'm what you might call a detective for hire. I don't work with an official outfit, but, let's say, people pay me to get things done when the police show incompetence. Some call me an assassin, hit man, I'm not one for titles."

My father glided through the barn, scanned the weapons, and his mouth almost hit the floor. "How long you been doing this gig?" he asked.

"Shortly after I met Samantha. There were a couple related murders in LeClaire and the police couldn't stop the killer. I witnessed one murder and victim related to Samantha. My business partner John and I took matters into our own hands. Samantha hired us to find the killer. You could say the side business kind of found me."

My father looked me up and down, and grimaced, his grey eyebrows pointing in, "How does an antique collector turn into an assassin? You're not a trained killer," he said.

"I trained with Navy Seals. Right before being deployed to the Middle East I tore an ACL.

Discharged, and that's the end. I don't like to talk about it," I said.

My father walked around the barn, picked up a rifle, and held it up with his eye over the scope. He shook a vial of poison, opened the cap, and smelled the contents. He pulled a knife from its sheath and touched the blade. "Why don't you want to talk about the military? That's a noble thing. I could've used you in my past. Samantha know about the side gig?"

I stumbled over my words knowing Sam didn't love the side business, "Kinda, but, John and I run things. She's good with Antique Adventures, but the killing business, not so much. She wants me to quit. Said the first job was to help her family only, and I needed to retire. But, I can't quit. You'd be surprised at the crime in LeClaire."

My father wiped sweat off his brow, "So, when you going to quit?"

I shook my head and frowned, "Not soon. Samantha doesn't know half of what goes on behind the scenes. I've tried to get out. But, it's harder than expected. Something keeps drawing me back."

"Remember my advice, son. You find a good woman you hang on for dear life. Don't mess this up."

I nodded, "I know, I will. Just not now."

My father laughed, "You must be an O'Kane. Once the crime bug gets in you it's hard to get out.

Most think people commit crime because they are evil and selfish. I think it's more about the rush and power you feel."

"I agreed on one level. But what I do is not crime. It's about justice and helping people. There's nothing more satisfying when a bad guy can't hurt innocent people any longer. I try to explain that to Samantha but she doesn't get it."

"Well, yeah, the justice thing too," my father said.

We both stood in the middle of the barn having a moment. Not talking, just thinking about how similar we are. I didn't know if there was anything my father and I could share. Maybe this was as close as we'd get. I'll take it.

Waved my dad over to a large desk and pushed a roller chair at his feet, "This is what I'll do. Offer you my services. John and I will put a strategy together to get your debts paid. I know you're broke, so this one is free," I said, with a wink.

My father shook his head side to side. "No, no, no. I'm not letting you get caught up with some Italian crime family. Anyone who threatens an old man for a thirty year old gambling debt has issues. I will just leave town and leave your family be."

I bent down in front of the roller chair and stared into his deep blue eyes, "I know you're hesitant. But I will save your life. We are the only protection you have in the world. I will make this problem go away. That's what I do."

My father grabbed my cheek and leaned in, "You're a young man, with a young family, and these men are dangerous. I'm old and don't have little in the tank. It's not worth putting yourself in harm's way. This is mine. I'll own it."

I pulled another chair over and sat back knowing he was right. I didn't want to put my family in harm's way. I knew I needed to quit the side business. But something was compelling me to help the father I barely knew. I kept hearing in my head the voice of an old lady teaching Sunday School, "Honor your father and mother." I couldn't think of a better way to obey this command. By saving his life.

George shot up from the roller chair and pushed it back under the table, "Dexter, I'm not okay with this. I don't need your help."

He disappeared back into the house.

# Chapter 12

I slouched in the swivel chair, spun around a couple times, and stared through the barn doors to the long driveway along the house. It was apparent my father didn't want my services, and I had the sense he didn't approve of the side business. He wanted to run. I wanted to run. Didn't know why I still wanted help save his ass but "honor thy father..." was strong in my head.

Picked at my cuticles and tried to collect my thoughts when a faint scream came from the front of the house. Paused, listened closely, and I heard it again. I pushed the swivel chair behind me with a leg whip and glided to the front of the barn.

A woman screamed.

I ran down the driveway and turned the corner at the front of the house to find George laying on the grass. A trickle of blood rolled down his right temple. Samantha knelt down next to him assessing the situation.

I jogged up next to the scene, "What the hell

happened?" I asked, Samantha wiping her hands on a dish rag.

Samantha held her hands over her mouth and tried to catch a breath, "I don't know. I heard commotion in the driveway and glanced up from slicing vegetables. A black car pulled up, a man jumped out, and rushed your dad. He didn't say a word and hit your dad with a bat in the face."

"You get a look at the attacker?" I asked.

"It happened so fast. The man was wearing some kind of black ski mask, jeans, and a hoodie. That's all I saw," Samantha said, wiping green peppers from her wet hands.

I gave Samantha a side hug, released her, and bent down over the body. I pressed my ear against dad's chest to listen for life. He coughed and opened his eyes. He gripped the side of his head and rolled side to side in pain, "My head is on fire. Did you get the guy with the bat?" he asked, eyes fluttering in and out of consciousness.

I shook my head no, "Shit, dad. This hasn't been your week. You get knocked out in the prison parking lot. And now a bat to the skull. Not what you envisioned entering back into civilization. Prison was safer," I said, with a smirk.

George grinned, slowly sat up, and held the side of his bleeding head, "I'll be fine. I put up my arm and deflected the blow from the bat. If you knew half the things in prison. This is a trip to the ice cream shop," he said, with a sigh.

I lifted my dad to his feet and assessed the wound. I wiped a piece of grass and dirt from his bloodied temple, "I think a little ice will do the trick. Sam, can you get ice from the freezer?" I asked.

I handed George off to Samantha and they walked back into the house while I stayed back in the yard. I walked to the street and looked in both directions hoping to see something. Not sure what.

I dialed my phone.

"John, Dex. Meet me at Common Grounds. We have work to do."

# Chapter 13

A blonde waitress hovered over our sticky table, snapped gum, and became impatient. I scanned the menu ignoring the snapping waitress. I couldn't decide between a Denver omelette or biscuits and gravy.

Smalley's is the best diner in LeClaire with its throwback charm. Waitresses dressed in 50's poodle skirts and black and white saddled shoes. Jukebox playing Chuck Berry. And, the best omelettes in the country. At least, that's what John, and I believed, not getting far outside Missouri. John and I have spent many hours plotting, dreaming, and scheming, in these booths over the last ten years.

"I'll do two eggs over-easy, side of bacon, and sourdough," I said, slamming down the plastic menu.

"Same. Can I get a refill on Diet Cherry Coke?" John asked.

The waitress blew a bubble, rolled her eyes, and rushed away with a sour look on her face.

"Let me get right to it. My father is in big trouble and needs our help," I said.

"Lester?"

"No, my real father."

John leaned over his almost empty Diet Cherry Coke and kept his eyes locked on me, "Your real dad? Isn't Lester your real dad?" John asked.

"He's my step dad. George's my biological dad. Just got out of Leavenworth two days ago. Staying at our place."

There's not much John and I don't know about one another. We have spent every moment of life from crib to present. It's rare to have friends like John. Connected at the hip. Yet this detail seemed to never come up.

John leaned forward from the red plastic booth making a sticking sound. He put his hands out in front of me trying not to spit out Coke through his nose, "Hold the phone, Dexter. Your dad is an ex-con? When were you going to tell me this big news," John asked, slurping the Coke dry.

I tried to compile a rational reason with little luck. It wasn't intentional. I had a stepfather, Lester, after my dad went to prison. My mother couldn't imagine being alone for the next thirty years, and I was little, and needed a daddy. At least that's what she told me.

"Our family closed the book on my dad after he

went to prison. Lester came into my life after my dad went away. I guess it didn't matter."

John tried to flag down the waitress to refill his drink with no luck, "Dude, two daddies? You're lucky. I would love one dad to stick around longer than an episode of Game of Thrones."

The truth is John had many daddies. He grew up in LeClaire with rotating fathers every couple of years. His first dad bailed after his mother got pregnant. Second a one night stand which lasted a couple years. Third dad hit his mom. Fourth, hit by a train, after drinking too much. John's mother liked the men. I'll leave it at that.

"His name's George. He got wrapped up with some Italian family, named the Buffone's. He owes them a lot of money from a gambling debt. They want the money or his head."

"Why does the family want money from a debt thirty years ago? That sounds fishy," John said.

"That's what I said. My dad killed one of their brothers when he was robbing a bank. They're mad."

John game me a face palm, "Wait. You have two dads and one of them is a thief and murderer. No way. That's awesome. I'd kill for one criminal dad... bad joke?"

I shook my head, "Let's stay focused on the mission, big fella."

Out of nowhere I choked up thinking about my mother. I avoided eye contact with John and watched a couple arguing in a table across the diner, "There's one more detail. My father ran a side business in prison to pay off his debts. It didn't work and someone had to pay," I put a hand on my forehead, "They killed my mother."

"Oh, shit. That's heavy."

"Yeah. Not the homecoming I was hoping for."

"What are we going to do?"

"The first plan of action is to figure out who we are dealing with. Is the Buffone family some kind of Italian mob? How dangerous are these chumps?"

John smirked, "Mob in LeClaire? That's funny."

The waitress came back to the table and slid our plates across the table. "Two eggs, bacon, and sourdough. Anything else you need?" she said, tossing the bill on the table.

"Nope," I said.

I held up a hand to my face and grabbed a piece of bacon with the other, "According to my father, this family are bad people. Still causing trouble in LeClaire."

"How are we going to find these guys? What you got?" John asked.

I reached down in the booth and pulled out a Macbook Air from my bag. I pressed the power button and heard the computer sing on, "A little tool I call Google."

John grinned, "Remember when we used the Yellow Pages to find an address? Feels like a million years ago."

I punched into the web browser Buffone Family LeClaire. The screen populated with search results. As I examined the screen, I felt a presence next to me.

A short man with dark slick hair in an Italian suit smiled back at me. He played with a tooth pick in his mouth, "Sorry to bother you, fellas. I won't take much of your time. My name is Mario and need a favor."

He reached out his hand to shake both of our hands. A sea of gold bracelets swung against his fury hands, "I'm a local business man and over-heard your conversation. It sounds like you're doing some kind of business on your own, am I right?" he said, with a smile revealing a gold tooth.

I stood and locked eyes with the Italian. I never liked when people get in my business when not invited, "Yes, we're doing business. But, none of your business. This is a private conversation. Can we get back to our food, thanks."

The mystery man held up his hands in inno-cence twirling a toothpick between his lips, "Easy tiger. I want no trouble. This won't take long."

I felt the entire diner staring in our direction. My boot nicked the shiny black dress shoes of the Ital-ian as I moved in closer, "Make this quick. I haven't finished my eggs."

The Italian leaned in and switched to a hushed tone whispering in my ear, "You scuffed my shoes. These Italian shoes are worth more than your life.

You don't want to get involved with people like myself. Someone will get hurt... Beginning with your wife, children, and your old man."

John rose from the booth. He adjusted his sweat pants and covered his gut hanging from under a Kansas State tee shirt. He put a sweaty hand on the man's shoulder, "We want to finish our breakfast. If I don't eat, I get ugly. I don't know who you are. But you need to leave right now. Or, we'll take this outside."

John stood six inches above the man and stared down on his slick black hair His face turned red. The thirty people in the diner locked on the commotion.

Silence.

The Italian slapped away John's hand. He pointed a finger up at John, "I'm serious, fellas. Be careful. You don't know who you're messing with."

John eased back.

The two men left the diner.

I felt my head get warm in embarrassment knowing everyone was staring at us. I addressed the diner, "Nothing to see here. Just a misunderstanding. Can you believe that guy?" I said, pointing at the glass front door of the diner.

John shook his head and sipped on his Coke trying to cool off. He glanced over at the menu tucked behind a napkin holder. He pulled it out and inspected.

"Check this Dex," John said, tapping on a small ad at the bottom of the page.

I picked up the menu and examined the ad. It was a sponsor with a picture of two Italian men smiling in front of a row of cars.

*Buffone Brothers Used Cars.*

# Chapter 14

Our Antique Adventures truck pulled into the Buffone Brother's Used Cars. John hopped out and ran in front of a green blowup man waving his arms. The foolproof marketing scheme of most used car lots in LeClaire. I wondered how effective the obnoxious waving man was for business. John amused.

"Check me out Dex," John said, mimicking the wind powered green man.

"Stop being an idiot. We got work to do. Let's go," I said, back handing John in his flabby midsection.

John made a face after I ruined his fun. We made our way through a pair of glass doors to the front office. A woman with too much makeup typed on a computer and didn't acknowledge two men hovering over her cluttered desk.

I whispered in John's ear, "Apparently a goldmine threw up on her neck."

The woman glanced up. I straightened up for

fear she heard my goldmine comment. "Can I help you sweetie?" she asked, applying red lipstick to her puffy lips.

I pointed across the lot to the Antique Adventures Ford F-150, "Yes, ma'am. My buddy and I are looking for a new work truck. A model with better fuel efficiency. The gas prices are killing us," I said, winking at John.

She nodded her head in agreement, "I feel your pain sweetheart. Business is bad of late. We're selling Asian economy cars these days. I even saw a contractor driving a Toyota Camry around town yesterday," she said, smacking a bright green piece of gum.

John played with a giant ball of rubber bands on her metal desk, "We need something with lots of cup holders. I drink a lot of soda," John said, jamming a large Big Gulp between his lips.

I elbowed John in the gut almost causing him to spew his sugar water on the white linoleum, "Don't listen to him. He doesn't leave the house much. You have a salesman we could talk with?"

She disappeared to a back office, and I spoke to John in a whisper, "Keep it cool, man. I'm trying to get a feel for the place. See if we can find a Buffone. Say no more stupid things."

I knew after the words left my mouth the probability of John filtering his words were slim to none. He got diarrhea of the mouth when things were tense, or new.

A greasy haired man came out of the office with a smile and a tooth pick in his mouth. The smell of cheap cologne punched us in the face. He stuck out a hand with a large gold ring on his pinky.

"Can I help you, paisano?"

I took off my hat and shook his hand, "I'm sorry, what does paisano mean?"

"Brother. It's Italian."

I looked over at John with a confused gaze, "Okay... I'm Irish, brother.

"It's what you say to friends," the Italian said.

"Well, thanks friend. We're looking for a new truck. Love the Ford. But need something a little easier on the pocketbook. Maybe a V-6 with better gas mileage?" I said, pointing to a line of trucks in the parking lot.

"You've come to the right place paisanos. I have just the right vehicle. It came in today," he said, waving us over to the glass doors.

We sauntered to the back of the car lot. He pointed to a new green Dodge Ram and explained all the features. "This is the model you need. Great gas mileage. All the bells and whistles. What you do for work?"

I looked at John and then back at the Italian, "We're antique dealers. We buy and sell rusty gold," I said, with a proud smile.

"You have a shop in town?"

"Nope. We sell our stuff online. eBay. Craigslist. Etsy."

He shook his head in agreement, "Internet where it's at. Many of our sales are coming from the Web these days. Customers know more about our cars than we do. Damn Google. Antique dealing sounds like interesting work. Any interesting finds?"

"Found a 1956 Chevy Truck in guys shed the other day. Worth twenty thousand. Antiquing pays the bills. But we also do other stuff on the side for extra cash."

"We all need other ways to make money. I'm not just a used car salesman. I have other irons in the fire. If you know what I mean?" he said, flipping around the toothpick in his lips.

I bumped his fist, "Between my kid's braces, all the home decorations my wife buys, who can afford it, right?"

We all laughed. "What kind of stuff you do on the side?" the Italian asked.

I stared at the name tag on his black suit. Joe Buffone. "I teach Karate," I said, throwing a chop into his neck and tossing him on the hood of a Ford Explorer. John scanned the parking lot making sure no one saw the altercation. It was empty with only the sound of the arm flapping green man pushing against the wind.

"Get off me," Joe said, his face turning bright red, tooth pick rolling off the hood of the car.

"I'm not your paisano. Have plenty of brothers. I don't like scum bags running around LeClaire threatening old men and their families. Sound familiar?" I said, pressing my forearm against his neck. Drool raced out of the side of his mouth onto the hood.

"You're crazy. Don't understand what you're talking about. I'm just a used car salesman."

I could feel the bones in his neck moving around under my forearm. He coughed trying to speak, "I want no trouble. I'll give you whatever you want. You like the Ram?"

I yanked the Italian from the hood of the Explorer, and ripped the name tag off his suit, and shoved it in his face. John came up behind the Italian and placed him in a choke hold, "You part of the Buffone mob family?"

"Yes, I'm a Buffone. My family owns the dealership. We're not out to hurt anyone... no mob people... just trying to make a living in LeClaire. I swear," he said, struggling for breath, getting redder, and sweat now streaming from each temple.

"Bull shit. You're making a living by cashing in on thirty-year-old debts from old men. You recall any bricks smashing through windows of late?"

Joe's face turned from red to blue with every added second of pressure, "No way. I know nothing about any old man, brick, or debts. Please paisano, let me go."

John pulled a vial from his back pocket and opened the top with a free hand. A small dropper emerged, "I promise this will not hurt," he said, placing a drop of the darkish liquid under the Italian's nose.

"What the hell are you doing? What is that shit?"

"Don't worry. You'll feel a fuzzy feeling in your mind, blurred vision, and darkness. We'll be gone when you awaken from your nap," John said, examining the liquid in the dropper, and squeezing it onto his face.

John released his forearm from the Italian's throat. He moaned and rubbed his neck, bent over in a heap, on the parking lot floor, "We'll call this a warning. If you get near me, my family, or hurt anyone close to me. The next darkness will be permanent."

Joe's body became limp and he slid facedown onto the cement, "Joe, I think we'll keep our truck for now," I said, winking at John.

# Chapter 15

The temperature dropped as the evening came closer. John sipped a Cherry Coke, and I held my iPhone up to my eyes over the steering wheel, "You believe that greasy Italian?"

John took another gulp, "I trust no one that wears that much gold. Between the receptionist and the salesmen we could pay our salaries for a year."

I pondered and thought about the denial of the salesman, "What if Joe didn't know what's going on? These Italian families can be large and maybe he's just a cousin, or something? He sounded sincere when I crushed his windpipe," I said, grinning at John.

John furrowed his brow and I could tell his small brain wheels were turning. "Wait, a minute. You remember Lenny from high school? The Italian kid in homeroom senior year," John asked.

"The one who ate meatball sandwiches every day at lunch, so what?"

"Wasn't his last name Buffone? I think his family owned the Italian joint on Main Street. The only one in LeClaire."

I glanced at John who was staring at the celling and licking his lips, "What is wrong with you?"

"I was thinking about meatball sandwiches. You hungry?"

I ignored the rumbling stomach of my fat partner, "I'll be honest. Don't remember high school all that much. Dated Lisa senior year, we married the next year, and drank a lot of beer in between. It all runs together. Kind of blur for me," I said.

John fiddled with his smartphone and Googled Lenny Buffone. A Facebook profile page populated on the small screen. "How did anyone stalk another person before Facebook? I'm old enough to remember life before computers and social media. The good ole days when you talked to people face-to-face. And had real friends not ones in cyberspace," John said, flashing the phone in my face.

I leaned in to get a better look at the profile picture.

"The Buffone family rumored to be part of the mob or something. All the kid's dressed well and lived in a big house up on Eagle Ridge Hill. I always thought it was an urban legend that kid's in LeClaire talked about in school because of boredom. But..." John paused, scratched his head, and set the phone in his lap.

"What is it, big fella?" I asked.

"I have a vague memory of Randy Brooks telling me during Chess Club about the new gymnasium that was being built senior year. The Buffone family were main contributors for the project. Nobody believed the revenue from a small Italian restaurant could support a multimillion dollar gym," John said.

"The Buffone family built that thing? That's where I met Lisa for the first time. At a basketball game," I said, with a grin.

"When you sat in the rafters and drooled over Lisa's cheerleading outfit? The uncoordinated creepy Irish kid," John said.

"Easy, I tried out for the team. Sports were not my thing. I still got the girl, right?"

"Whatever it takes, stalker," John said.

"Anyway... Back to the Buffone's. The only people living in LeClaire with that kind of cash are doctors, lawyers, or in the mob," I said.

LeClaire never considered a cultural hub in Missouri. We have our annual BBQ competition, country fair comprising a few rides and petting zoo, and an average minor league baseball team, the T-Bones. Not the place of mob work. I tried to wrap my head around the Buffone's working an underground crime ring and it made little sense.

John slammed his hand on the dashboard hitting a pine tree air freshener on the way down. It swung side to side and blinded my view through the truck windshield.

"Settle down big guy. We'll get 'em," I said, grabbing the air freshener.

"If the high school stories are true. It makes total sense. There's no reason NOT to believe the Buffone's are after your father," John said, staring out the passenger window.

I still had my doubts.

"But the Buffone's own a used car dealer not a restaurant. You think it's a front?" I asked.

"Remember what Joe said when we kicked the crap out of him. Everyone has side jobs for money," John said, raising an index finger.

"That could mean anything, Sherlock," I said.

My phone rang and Samantha was on the other line. She was in a panic, "Someone broke into the house when I was at the store. Your father's gone," she said.

I hung up and looked over at John, "The Buffone's are at it again," I said, jamming in the gas pedal.

# Chapter 16

John followed close behind onto the porch. I yanked a Beretta .92 out of the back of my jeans. The screen door hung by a thread and swung in the breeze. "Samantha? You in there?"

She appeared from the kitchen wearing yoga pants and a Kansas City Royals baseball hat pulled low on her face. She jumped into my arms cutting the circulation from my neck. I whispered in her ear. "You okay? How are the babies?"

"We're fine. But I'm not liking any of this..."

I unlocked Samantha's death grip and set her down in the middle of the living room. The remnants of a glass coffee table laid at our feet. A wooden rocking chair flipped on the side and books were strewn on the floor at the base of a white bookcase.

I knelt down and placed a book back in the shelf. "This stuff can be replaced. I'm glad everyone's okay."

I glided down the hall, pulled the Beretta out,

and raised it to eye level. I gently pushed a bedroom door open where my father stayed.

I peered in.

A mattress was flipped up against the far wall and laid on top of a low dresser. Clothes, antiques, and papers were thrown across the small bedroom. I looked to the right where a mirror was hanging half-cocked and cracked in the middle. I saw the opposite wall in its reflection.

I paused.

In large red spray painted letters: *We need our money.*

I called John and Samantha from the other room. They rushed in, John huffing from the short journey. I pointed to the wall.

"That's not good. You think it's the Buffone family?" John said, catching his breath.

"Who is the Buffone family?" Samantha asked, examining the mess in the bedroom.

"The people who are after dad. We think an Italian family might be trying to kill him," I said, leaning into the spray painted wall.

"We might have found a clue from a meeting we had earlier today. I remember the Buffone name from high school back in the day," John said.

Samantha ran out of the room like something was burning on the stove. She came back with a high school yearbook and flipped frantically through the pages. Scanning the pages up and down her finger slammed down on a brown haired girl. "Is this chick part of the same family?"

I squinted to read the small print on the shiny page. "Oh, shit. Elizabeth Buffone. Did you have classes with her?" I asked, reading the front of the yearbook.

"Not only did we have classes together. She goes to my yoga classes on Wednesday mornings."

John ripped the book out of my hand and found the picture of Elizabeth. "Let me see this chick. Nope, doesn't ring a bell."

John didn't know many girls in high school. Let's just say he played a lot of Dungeon and Dragons. What he called a *thinking* sport.

"Although, Elizabeth is not a Buffone anymore. She's a Wilson. Married a cop, I think," Samantha said.

"A cop?" I asked.

"Yep. LeClaire PD. The counties finest," Samantha said, with a grin.

"You don't think the cops are involved? I know LPD doesn't have the best reputation?" I said.

John explored the thrashed bedroom and played with the remnants of an antique on the floor. He picked up a silver horse missing the head and examined it. "Why is a gambling debt from thirty years ago so important? Why would police be involved? If this family are true thugs, why spend all the energy on an old man, and get LPD involved?" John asked.

"That's what we're going to find out," I said.

The doorbell rang and a voice yelled from the front porch. "LeClaire PD. We got a call from this address."

We all looked at one another and smiled. "Perfect timing," I said.

# Chapter 17

I met the cops at the screen door and tried to hang it back on the frame.

"Hello, sir. Sorry we have to meet again on such short notice. I'm Brown and this is Metcalf. Looks like you had an intruder," said the flat-topped officer examining the broken screen door.

"Think so," I said.

"We got a call..." looking down at a note pad, "From a Samantha O'Kane? A break in..."

Nodded my head in agreement. "I think those kids are up to no good again," I said, with a nervous smile.

I led them to the bedroom. The smaller officer peeked over my shoulder at the destroyed room and made a couple notes on his pad. "Looks like this might be more serious than a rock through a window."

My wife ran into the room and talked fast. "Thanks for coming officers..." I held a hand to silence her, "We're taking care of it dear," I said, giving her a look.

She waved at the officers. "I'll let my husband handle it."

Both officers looked at one another and shrugged their shoulders. "Tell me Mr. O'Kane. Was anyone home or hurt during the break in?"

"Nope. We were getting lunch, came home, and welcomed by this mess. Dang kids," I said, snapping my fingers.

"Everybody's okay, correct?" asked the flat-topped officer.

"Yes, sir. Everyone is doing great. Just a little mess to clean up. No big deal. My entire life is about cleaning up messes, right?" I said, slapping the officer on the arm.

The other officer looked me up and down. "Are you okay, sir? You seem nervous."

"I had a lot of caffeine at lunch. Those free refills at Smalley's. You gotta get your monies worth."

The flat top officer looked over my shoulder with an eyebrow raised. "Where's the old man who was here last time? He okay?"

"Um, well, he's in the back taking a nap. After coming home and seeing the mess he needed to lie down. Normal old people stuff. He takes a nap every day at four. Got to have it or he's a bear," I said, with a wide grin.

The officers shook their heads up and down.

"You mind if we have a look around rest of the house?"

I stuck out my arm almost poking one officer in the chest. I looked back at John. "We're fine officers, really. Just a bunch of kid's pulling a prank. Nothing stolen, nobody hurt, we're fine," I said, giving a stare.

"I don't want to be rude, sir. But you're acting strange for a man whose home broken into. Are you sure you don't want to file a report?"

I shook my head side to side. The sweat from the lies formed on my back. "Nothing stolen. A few things broken, nothing that can't be replaced," I said, glancing back at the broken coffee table.

"No report?" the officer asked scratching his head.

"Unnecessary," I said.

The two officers turned to one another, scrunched their faces, and then back at me. "Okay. Well, ugh, if you will not file a report, and will not let us look around, we'll leave. Call the department if you need any other help."

The officers turned and walked away and were about to open the cruiser doors. I walked to the edge of the porch. "Before you go. I know this is random. You guys know an officer Wilson? He's part of LPD?" I asked.

Both the officers smiled on cue and answered in harmony. "He's the Police Chief. Why?"

I saluted the men. "No big deal. Just trying to track down an old friend. Have a good day," I said.

The police cruiser disappeared as the sun set over Missouri.

# Chapter 18

The alarm clock glowed midnight. A late night for a family with three small children. I stared at the spinning ceiling fan casting shadows against the light Samantha used to read her book. She devoured romance novels like mice on cheese.

I could sense an unspoken tension between us. With, revelation of my father who she didn't know existed weeks earlier. The Buffone family. We weren't connecting.

I rolled to my side. "Sweetie. Can we talk?"

Samantha turned a page on the novel and didn't look in my direction.

Stoic. Emotionless face.

"Maybe."

"I know you're deep into your book. But can I have a second to chat?" I said, leaning on my side.

She placed the book face down on top of the flowery comforter staring straight ahead.

I touched her chin and tried to nudge it toward

my unshaven face. "Sweetheart. I'm sorry. I haven't been honest the last few days."

Silence.

My apology falling flat on the floor like a balloon losing its helium.

Samantha leaned over to a brown nightstand and placed her book on a stack of other romance novels. She turned back.

"I'm sorry too."

I shot up almost ripping the covers from the bed. Raised an eyebrow. "Why are you sorry?"

She grabbed my hand and gave it a gentle kiss. I could feel tingles shoot through my body. "When I found out about your dad, I was mad. I want our marriage to be an open book where we can share everything. But... I realized... this is painful for you. I had a great dad and don't know what it's like to live with this kind of void. Sorry for not being more understanding and patient with you," she said, giving me another kiss on the cheek.

I smiled and felt more tingles coursing through the man region. "This might be the easiest make-up-sex ever."

Samantha punched me in the arm. "Seriously, Dexter. You're such a man."

I leaned in and grabbed the side of her face. "I want to apologize for not being honest. This part of my story is difficult to talk about. I don't know how I should feel about my father, who I thought was dead, mind you. I thought it would feel different."

"A lot has happened in the last couple years. Your wife and kid's death, a new wife, three new kids, and a new business. Sometimes it's hard to know what normal life's supposed to be like," Samantha said, caressing my chest.

"I wonder if there's too many years between dad and I to have a normal relationship."

"Time will tell."

"You think we need to worry about the Buffone family? They're harmless Italians, right?"

Samantha rubbed my chest and kissed my neck and gave me the look. "There's nothing to worry about. You're my strong man. I know you and John will figure it out."

The tingles were strong. "I never want to lie to you again. No matter what. Okay. We good?"

We pulled the covers over our heads and made love. I couldn't shake feelings of how little Samantha knew me.

My entire life felt like a lie.

# Chapter 19

The barn smelled of wood and must. Remnants of spring rains moving toward a dry summer still lingering in the turn of the century farm house. I unclamped the padlock and slid the large barn doors squeaking with age.

"I can't believe Samantha let me refinish this place," I said to John.

John shook his head knowing I was lucky to have a supportive wife like Samantha.

Last year's revenue from Antique Adventures made the barn a usable space for the side business. The former home of mooing cows and clucking chickens. Now furnished with computers, whiteboards, desks, refrigerator (for adult beverages), and bathroom with full shower. The tools needed to catch bad guys.

I picked up a Dry Erase marker and drew a large circle in the middle of the whiteboard. I then wrote: The Buffone Family.

Protruding from the circle lines in every direction. At the end of each line: Dad, Elizabeth, used car salesman, Chief of Police, someone inside prison working with dad, high school gym.

I paced the barn feeling like a professor in a room full of eager students. The only learner being John. "This is what we got. Each line represents a piece of the puzzle. Our job is to make the connections and finish the puzzle."

John meditated on the whiteboard for a moment. You could see the wheels turning in his brain. He pointed at the middle of the board. "I think we can say with certainty the Buffone family is part of this mess. The high school connection, the car salesman, Elizabeth, the gym, and now the Chief of Police. And, not to mention, there aren't many Italian families in LeClaire," John said, with a grin, sipping a beer in a rubber can coozie.

I slammed my fist against the board for effect. "Yes! We need to figure out the Chief of Police connection. If Elizabeth's maiden name is Buffone. Her husband is head of the LeClaire PD and this family is dangerous. Where there's smoke there's always fire," I said, sitting back in a leather chair and chewing on a marker.

John walked over to a computer station and pecked at the keyboard. A series of numbers and formulas danced across the thirty-two inch monitor. "Come check out my latest creation," he said, with excitement.

I glanced over Big John's shoulder and pretended to look interested. I nodded and smiled. "So... what are we looking at? Numbers and squiggles give me rashes and remind me of math class."

"What's our motto?"

"Beware of Chinese buffets. Especially, ones owned by Texans."

"No, idiot. Kill clean. Kill last."

John and I didn't get into the business because we're monsters with an agenda to kill. Our foray into the assassination gig found us. My wife's family caught up in a string of murders, and we stepped in. We wanted to protect Samantha and LeClaire. At least that's what we told ourselves. Our joy is not in the kill. Our joy is justice.

"Kill last." Do our best to kill as last resort. "Kill clean." Kill with dignity and don't allow people to suffer... unless necessary.

John grabbed my head and stared at the top of my short brown hair. He tapped like knocking on a door.

"Ouch. What are you doing?" I yelled.

"Your brain is smaller than most. But most brains are fascinating animals that act like computers. Every vein, vessel, and function moving along through this spongy three pound glob. It hums along like an oiled machine," he said, as he tapped the side of my head.

"Can you stop now?"

John pushed me back and continued his lecture. "I think I have come up with a way to shut down this computer using magnets and electricity. I'm using magnetic beams which create electricity to shut off portions of brain activity. It's called transcranial magnetic stimulation, and is being studied in the UK, it's highly controversial. But I think if I experiment with it we can use it for the biz. Painless and clean."

I nodded and smiled at the invention. "Isn't this just a glorified taser? Police carry these all the time."

"Tasers don't kill people. At least they aren't supposed to. It still needs work. I need more power to shut the brain down," John said, with a grin.

John was a computer science major at Missouri State before switching to biology. He hoped to be a doctor. That was until he realized smart people don't always work well with others in structured situations. He dropped out junior year after too many experiments and not enough studying. The Smartest guy I know.

"How does this help our current case?"

He tapped at the computer and moved the mouse on the brown desktop. "If I can get more power through the magnets, we'll be amazed at what this technology can do. We can take out a bad guy from yards away with little effort. Humans are great conductors of electricity, you know?"

"Okay Inspector Gadget. Keep working on the taser and I'll think about next steps."

John shook his head, "It's not a... never mind."

I stood at the entrance of the barn and breathed

in the warm Missouri air. I couldn't stop thinking about my dad and what someone might do to him. Deep down I wanted my father back in my life. But not under these circumstances.

I turned back and shouted to John sitting at the desk. "You keep working. We need to find my father. Where you think a mob family would hang out?"

# Chapter 20

The sound of dripping water echoed in a damp room. George didn't know direction of the voices mumbling in the distance. He said a prayer not sure if death was knocking at the door.

Dexter's father caressed with the back of one hand a swelling, throbbing pain in his face. Someone had punched or kicked him repeated times. He examined the blood running from the corner of his mouth and felt his eye swelling with every agonizing minute.

A gush of hot air grazed his cheek, "So, you get thrown in the slammer and think all debts cancelled. You murder family and think we forget. This is not a get-out-of-jail-free card in a game of Monopoly. Think again, George O'Kane."

George aware he was gagged and mumbled incoherent sounds under the rag. He kept speaking. A man ripped duct tape from his mouth and the stickiness took lip with it, "Let's hear what you have to say" said the mystery man, in a thick Italian accent.

George strained to hold his head up feeling the back muscles tighten from being punched and hit in the spine. Blindfolded he only could hear voices, "I did everything I could from the inside. I'm sorry the plan fell apart, and the debts weren't paid. I was in prison for thirty years. What was I supposed to do?"

He felt a presence nudge close to his body and whisper, "That's why your wife got killed."

George could feel a tear welling up on his swollen face. A drop of blood dripped in time with the dripping water pipes. He didn't speak.

Another voice came from behind him. A sound echoing off the cement floor made it seem the man wearing large work boots.

"Hello, Georgie-boy. It's not important you know my name at this point. But, you will in time. I'm a vital contributor to the community of LeClaire. The people of LeClaire are like family entrusted into my care. I work hard each day making sure people treated fairly, are safe, and any evildoers punished for their crimes. I don't like hearing about thugs, like yourself, not paying back their debts, and hurting innocent people. Like your wife."

George hung his head as the pain in his neck was too strong, "I'm an old man. I did my time. You made me kill my wife, and you know it. I need not relive this hell. Why are you doing this?"

The man grabbed George's hair and yanked his head back. He could feel hair follicles coming out of their sockets, "Listen. We don't need your sob story. The men standing behind me are essential to the economy and wellbeing of LeClaire. When people don't pay their debts everyone suffers. You don't want the people of LeClaire to suffer because you won't pay back the money, do you?"

George hesitated and tried to speak which came out cracked, "How much?"

The sound of mumbling voices echoed through the cold and dark room. "How much is the wellbeing of LeClaire worth to you?"

"Depends who you ask."

"Oh, a smart ass. I thought you born and raised here? That doesn't sound like a response, from a man who loves his place of origin."

"I have little family left."

"If you don't care that much. Let's say, one million will do."

"Kill me."

"What's that old man?"

"Kill me. I'm fresh out of prison, no prospects, and no money. Take the debt out of my ass."

Laughter filled the room, "Funny guy. We wouldn't let you get off that easy. You have one week to get us the money. Or, we'll take it out of an ass. Dexter's ass."

"Don't you dare hurt my son. Kill me. Leave him out of this. This is not his problem."

"We know he does well with his junk collecting business. I think we'll see if he can pay your debts. Since you're not that interested in the community of LeClaire."

George whimpered and cried out. "Please... kill me... not Dexter."

Silence.

George felt arms surrounding his feeble body and the next thing he knew he was tumbling out onto a lawn.

Dexter's lawn.

# Chapter 21

I stared at the evidence of our case on the wall of the barn. Photos of Elizabeth, Chief of Police, dad, used car salesman, looking back at me. I tapped a pencil on the desk and leaned back in my swivel chair.

The sound of tires squealed in the distance. John looked in my direction and we ran out of the barn. We found George tied up on the front lawn, gag in mouth, with a note pinned to his green polo shirt.

I grabbed my gun from the back of my jeans and glanced up and down our country gravel road.

No one.

I raised my father up and untied the gag. I examined the note.

We need one million dollars for unpaid debts. Next time your father won't live.

My father sat up leaning against my leg. He didn't make a sound.

"Who did this to you?"

He shrugged his shoulders.

"You get a look at anybody?" He shook his head side-to-side mouthing no.

I placed the note in my back pocket, put my father in the house to clean him up, and bandaged his wounds. His face cut up bad, a couple scrapes were on his legs, and I got ice for the swelling.

I filled the bathtub with warm water, stripped my father naked, and helped his broken body into the soothing water. He grimaced as he sank deeper into the tub.

He stayed silent.

I washed the mixture of dirt and blood off my father's body. Rage rumbled throughout my body.

The thought of dad in a scary place getting the shit kicked out of him was not a good image to have in my head. I underestimated the love a son could have for their absent father. I always saw my stepfather as not the real thing. A good man. But, not my real dad.

I rubbed a wash cloth across my father's face trying to clean out the wounds. I never imagined meeting my real dad let alone nursing him back to health. A tear trickled down my cheek.

"Don't worry dad. We'll fix this."

He nodded and stayed silent sinking into the tub.

# Chapter 22

It was 3 PM, an afternoon breeze swept through the backyard of the house. We sat huddled around a bonfire on the back patio. My father curled up in a patio chair with a blanket engulfing his wounded skinny body.

"How are the battle wounds dad?" I asked.

"I'm okay. But there's one thing," he said, staring in the distance like thinking hard on a math equation.

"What ya need?"

"A cell phone."

I didn't think the request was unreasonable. I considered the kidnapping and the need to keep an eye on an old man who was being watched by the Italian mafia, "That's not a bad idea."

My father leaned into the bonfire and warmed his hands with blanket draped over his skinny shoulders, "I was thinking after the incident yesterday a phone might be good to keep in touch. In case I get in trouble and need help. I will not lie, those guys scared me yesterday."

I nodded in agreement.

Temperatures in the backyard dropped and sounded like an excuse for a trip to Spunky's. The oldest chain of grocery stores in Missouri. The all-in-one stop for groceries, yard supplies, and electronics. If you can't find it at Spunky's, it doesn't exist.

We loaded into the truck and made the fifteen minute drive to the store. I watched the sunset and contemplated the ability to love the man sitting next to me. A few weeks ago, I didn't know he existed. Now I had feelings reserved only for blood of my blood. I still had reservations of being okay with the situation. But this is where we were. And I had to deal.

The automatic glass doors flung open, and we veered left to electronics. I leaned on the glass case and peered into the sea of cell phones. An over-weight woman appeared from a back stock room. "The last guy who dirtied my case lost a finger. Can I help you?"

I gave a half smile not sure if this was a joke or Missouri banter. I banked on the former. "Yes. We need a new cell phone. You got any of those pay-as-you-go disposable ones? I don't know how long this old guy will be around," I said, elbowing my dad in the gut. He did not find the joke amusing.

The woman gave a sigh and annoyed stare like

she'd been working at Spunky's five years too long. She yanked on a string of keys protruding from her wide hips, unlocked the case, and slid open the back panel. She placed three phones on the glass top like dealing cards.

"These are the pay-as-you-go models you're looking for. There's a $20, $30, and $40 option. Each one with a couple more features" she said, staring over our heads thinking about a different job.

My father pointed at the cheapest option. "This one's fine. We only need it for calls. Texting, email, and all that other stuff, will just overwhelm him." I said, patting the top of his thinning hair.

We paid for the phone and waited on a bench for the unpleasant worker to program the new number. "You have been quiet since the kidnapping. What's on your mind?" I asked, my father fiddled his thumbs and stared at the floor.

"When tied to that chair I couldn't stop thinking about prison. It represents all the stupid shit I did, and the pain I caused you, mom, and everyone around me. Every day, you're faced with life and death. You don't want to piss off the wrong people or you'll get the shit kicked out of you... or something worse. You don't want to know what worse is."

"I can't imagine. Probably not pretty."

"If I'm honest. Wanted to die in that damp room

with those thugs. I don't know what else there's to live for."

I put my arm around my father, pulled him close, and could feel the bones in his frail shoulders crack. "You're safe now. We will make sure no one hurts you and all debts paid. There's still a lot of life to live here in LeClaire."

He nodded as the cell phone lady called over with the activated phone. She gave us the new number and my dad stared at the phone laughing. "I realized this is my first cell phone."

I smiled and showed him how to make and receive calls. "Welcome to the modern world."

"Not sure if I like this new world."

"You okay staying right here for a few minutes? I need to get a couple groceries before we head home. Samantha needs bread and milk."

My father raised his hand in agreement. "Take your time. I need to figure out this new contraption and make a call anyhow."

I headed toward the groceries section in the back of the giant all-in-one store.

George wandered around the front of the store and pulled out a number on a piece of paper in his pocket. He made his first call.

"Hello? Is this Peter?" The deep voice confirmed it was on the other end. "He knows nothing. You can reach me at this number from now on. When do you want to meet?"

I came back and found my father sitting on the

same bench in front of the cell phone area. I handed him the bag of groceries. "Who were you talking to? You said you needed to call someone?"

He gave me a half smile, "Oh, no one. Just an old friend."

# Chapter 23

I got up the next morning feeling better about things. Sipped my coffee and pulled into the parking lot of Antique Adventures. John's Honda Civic parked in a front space with "Vice President" on a hand painted wooden sign. He thinks titles are important because he says he gets no respect.

I expected the front door to be locked of the store because it was before hours. It wasn't. "John-O, where you at?"

John appeared from a back office and smiled back at me. "I've not heard name since high school."

I turned on an iMac computer in the front of the store. "Where's Amy?"

John shrugged.

Amy was the intern. We hired her to learn the ropes of the business and help find picking spots in Missouri and the greater Midwest. She was a whiz on the computer and a failure at punctuality. Typical college student.

"Well, since Amy is not here yet. Let's do freestyling this morning. We need money after a couple days off."

Freestyling is my favorite kind of picking. It brings out the adventure of why we got into the business. The unknowns. Crazy people you might meet. Danger.

The strategy of freestyling is simple. Drive the back roads of Missouri while investigating barns, sheds, or anything that might be suitable for financial gain. Walk up to the house (if there is one), introduce yourself, and hand them a flyer of all the items we are looking for. If they oblige, you jump into their rusty gold, and hope for the best. I won't say it's better than sex, but the high lasts longer.

John ran a flyer through the copy machine and handed me a stack of twenty. "Let's go. I'm feeling lucky today."

We headed through the winding hills of highway 50. A long stretch of road along the highway were littered with barns, sheds, and run down property. These areas have proven to be successful in the past. We drove down the quiet highway my mind racing back to George. How were we to find his kidnappers? Pay his debts?

John sipped on a Diet Cherry Coke. "Any ideas on how to find your fathers kidnappers? Pay his debts?"

"What the hell? You read minds?"

"No. But I have known you since the womb and I know the look."

"What look?"

John took a deep sip on the Coke the straw telling him it was gone. "That look when you are thinking about stuff you don't want to talk about. That look when you're trying to figure out a plan. You know, that Dexter look. I'm no dummy."

They say married couples can read each other's minds when they are together for a long time. I don't know if it's true, but it's true for John and I.

"I'm just a little worried about my dad. Not sure what to do at the moment."

"Everything will be fine."

"You kidding me right now? That seems like a flippant answer after my father just got the shit beaten out of him. And, the wannabe Italian mafia wants a million bucks out of his ass."

"I meant..."

Sometimes John's responses to tense situations are not what they seem. He's as laid back as a long LeClaire summer. John the optimist I'm the pessimist. I worry, and he believes everything will work out. We are very different. But, I've seen more shit in my life, to not put faith in humanity, or myself.

"You know what I mean, right? We always think of something. Can we talk about something else? I'm out of Coke and need food," John said, holding up his empty Diet Cherry Coke.

"How do you drink that sugar water first thing in the morning?"

"Like my dad used to say when asked how to get to Carnegie Hall. Practice, practice, practice."

"Well, let's pretend for a moment, your Coke is full, and you'll give actual solutions, to actual problems. How might you solve my father's dilemma?"

John grabbed one of his many chins and took a Thinking-Man pose. "I think whoever is behind this, are bluffing. They are a bunch of old, washed up thugs trying to make a quick buck off an old man, who's irrelevant to this whole thing. They need money and your dad is the scapegoat."

I shook my head up and down, stared out the front windshield at the empty highway, and thought about the response.

"What if the Italians are for real? What if my dad still owes these debts and they will get paid no matter what? Out of dad's ass... my ass... or your ass...What then?"

"What then? We do what we always do. We take them out."

I smiled and reminisced on the serial killer we laid down a couple years ago. Turns out that's how I met my wife. Long story. I couldn't believe our side business would protect the people of LeClaire from the darkness no one wants to admit exists. Not even our own families know extent of our side hustle. Or, the shady shit in LeClaire.

"Can you be specific?"

John ignored the question. "Let's focus on the pick, Dex. We'll figure it out, I promise. Don't worry...be happy."

"It would be nice not to have a care in the world like you big fella. How do you do it?"

"It's more art than science."

We spent the morning knocking on doors, handing out flyers, winning some, and losing some. The truck filled with old gas pumps, bicycles, rusty tools, and a couple signs. Not a bad day of freestyling.

A few hours later, after loading the warehouse with rusty gold, I made it home. I opened the door and found a note on the kitchen counter.

"Dexter, I'm taking the twins to my mothers. I don't want to be around you, your father, and the chaos right now. I'll call in a couple days when I'm ready. Please don't visit. – Samantha."

Dammit, slamming my fist on the granite counter. My father's homecoming is making things more complicated than expected.

# Chapter 24

S teve Miller Band played on the jukebox at O'Malley's pub. The gentle buzz of a joint, smoked a few hours earlier, coursed through my veins. It had been a couple years before my last toke. The habit originating after the death of Lisa and Spencer.

Deserved a little numbing this day.

I tapped obviously on the slick bar top getting the bartenders attention. Ordered my usual Jack and Coke. More Jack than Coke. Another first, after a couple years of AA meetings, and steering clear of liquid courage.

"Tell me young man. What's your family like?" I asked Marty, the owner of O'Malley's since the 80's.

Marty smiled and cleaned out a beer glass. "You drunk, Dexter? I haven't seen you in here since Lisa and Spencer."

In small towns everyone knows your name. Which includes when wife and son killed in car accidents. It's endearing and annoying when you're trying to escape life for the moment.

I stirred my red straw and popped a peanut in my mouth chewing the shell and all. "Maybe I'm drunk. Maybe just avoiding family. They're all nuts, you know?" I said, in a slow slur.

The bartender placed the cleaned glass under the bar and poured more peanuts in my empty basket. "My family has its issues. Probably not any more crazy than yours. I have an uncle did time for molesting kids."

I laughed and downed a big gulp of Jack and Coke burning the back of my throat. "My dad molested children..." shaking my head in confusion, "I mean, he was in prison, too."

"See, all families are nuts. What did your pops do time for?"

"He robbed a bank and killed someone," I said, with my chest protruding with pride. "I bet my dad can beat up your dad."

"Told, ya. All families are crazy." The bartender laughed and was done with my drunken ramblings. He walked down the bar and focused on a less drunk customer.

I sat at the same barstool the day of Lisa and Spencer's funeral. John didn't want me to leave the funeral that day. But I did. Not all lost. Met Samantha later in this same bar. Love that girl.

Called Marty over for another drink. A breeze on my neck as the door to the bar swung open. A woman and man stumbled in laughing and holding one another. I didn't get a good look too focused on my drink.

"I used to have that kind of love with my wife...both wives," I said, turning around on the barstool. The couple was in the back booth chatting like best friends and laughing with red faces.

I raised my glass toward the couple. "To love."

My eyes refocused and caught a better glimpse of the couple. My heart pounded. It was Samantha. I stood up and stumbled over to the red booth.

I hovered over the table, stood for a second, before they realized I was standing in front of them. Samantha caught me on a glance and stopped laughing.

"Hello wife," I said, slurping on my tiny red straw trying to look tough. To no avail. Ice popped over the rim of the glass and landed on the lap of the man.

He leapt up from the table like being stung by a bee, "What the hell buddy? You have a problem?"

"I do buddy. This is my wife. What the hell are you doing here with her? We met at this fine establishment. Let's finish this in the parking lot," I said, not sure where to point for the parking lot.

He raised his hands and didn't want to fight. The man crept back into the booth. I reached over the table, and grabbed his black buttoned up shirt by the collar, and drug him by the neck and stood him to his feet.

I pushed him back and stabbed his chest with my index finger. He continued to raise his hands up in the air. I yanked on his collar and dragged his resistant body toward the parking lot. "What in the hell are you doing with my wife? She's mine asshole."

"I don't want to fight man. You're drunk. Why not sleep it off?"

"Yes, you're making true statements. I have smoked and drank a lot tonight. But, I will still kick your ass. My drunkenness will make it a fair fight. No one messes around with my wife."

With no warning I punched him square in the nose. Blood spewed onto the dirt and gravel parking lot floor. The man fell to his knees grasping his bloody face. "Please man. No more. It's not what you think. You already broke my nose."

I kicked him in the side of the head with my leather boots. He tipped over like a crumbling building in a heap and writhed on the ground. "Please..."

I punched and kicked the man losing sight of time and reality. He laid in the fetal position and made no noise. His cries for help were background noise, and I didn't know where I was. A movie played in my mind of the vague memories of my father pushing me on a swing in the park. Two caskets enter the ground in a cemetery. I said, "I do," on my wedding day with Lisa and Samantha. I punched, kicked, cried, and didn't feel a thing.

Paused for a moment, and stood over the body,

like Muhammad Ali defeating George Foreman. A hand grabbed the back of my shirt. I turned to see Samantha crying and yelling to stop. I couldn't hear the words and only read her lips.

I stepped back, glanced down at the man bleeding, and wiped a small trickle of blood from the corner of my mouth. The one punch he got in. "No one messes around with my wife, asshole," I said, with a grin.

Samantha crumpled over the body and cried. He moaned and spilled blood over the dirt and our shoes.

"What got into you, Dexter? I'm not sleeping with this guy, asshole."

"You shouldn't be here with him. I know you're mad, but we can work it out. We always do."

She stood up from the man with tears streaming down her face.

"I'm not on a date. He's my brother. He's in town."

# Chapter 25

T he house was dark and quiet for the first time in a couple years. I paced the living room trying to make sense of the bar incident. My family was dysfunctional enough. Didn't have room for a brother-in-law who I didn't know existed until today.

Held my phone horizontal, and I spoke into the speaker continuing to pace, "I'm sorry about tonight. Wasn't in my right mind. But I thought we tried to live as open books. No secrets, apparently not."

The moment the words left my mouth I felt the thickness of hypocrisy dripping from every plea. Samantha didn't know half the stuff I've done or am doing (including the incarcerated father and side business that might involve killing bad guys).

Samantha said nothing and I could hear her calming the twins in the background. She came back on the line. "Before you go beating the crap out of people maybe you should ask a few more questions. You smoking pot again? Smelled it on your clothes at the bar."

I tried to dodge the question and focus on the argument at hand. My dabbling with pot and alcohol (again) would lead nowhere good with Samantha. When we met, I was in deep with these former loves.

"Let's not worry about the pot for a second. You need to tell me about this brother. Did you ever intend to let me know about the mysterious sibling?"

"Well Dex that makes two of us who had family in jail. I think we're even on that score."

"Jail? Your brother's a criminal?"

"Let's not talk about criminals. We both have no room to talk."

"True."

"So why is this jailbird hanging out with you? Are you at your mother's?"

"Yes. We will stay here for a while. My brother's been away for five years and we need to reconnect."

"What did he do?"

"Money laundering. He got caught up with some bad guys at his corporate job and things went south. He tried to make a little money on the side and it bit him."

"I know what that's like."

"What? Is there something you need to tell me?"

"That's not what I meant. I know what it's like to run a side bus- never mind."

I moved to the couch and sat in my dark living room. The only twinkle of light coming from the moon through the front window. It brought me back to the lonely and silent nights mourning the loss of Lisa and Spencer. A weight settled in my gut. The thought of losing Samantha, and the twins, step daughter, while not by death, felt the same.

"Can we please talk in person? I need to see you."

Silence.

Pleaded again, "Samantha, please. I screwed up with not telling you about dad. Beating the shit out of your brother was not right, either. But, please come home..." I said, as a small tear walked down my cheek, and bounced off the wooden coffee table.

"I need a little time. There's too much going on right now and I am not sure how I feel right now. I'll call you tomorrow."

"That's fair. Can you at least tell me the name of your brother?"

"Why?"

"Well, he's family. And, I probably should apologize."

"Peter."

"I'll wait for your call tomorrow."

"If I catch you with weed we're done."

"No problem. Done."

Samantha hung up the phone, and I reached

into my shirt and smoked another joint. Some things are hard to let go.

# Chapter 26

A Missouri breeze kicked up sand in the park sandbox. I placed the twins in a swing harness and pushed them to their delight. My step-daughter gave an occasional push.

Samantha relented and let me take the boys to Greenwood Park. My dad sat on an adjacent bench and smiled watching the boys and Lisa enjoy the sunny day and wind through their hair. For a moment it felt like a real family...except Samantha was missing.

"You want to go higher?" I asked, pushing the boys further than Samantha would be comfortable. I peeked out into a grass field next to the swings. A brown haired man wearing a flannel walked toward us. He waved his hand like we knew each other, and I gave a half-smile, confused.

The man came closer and I could see a bandage on his cheek.

It was Peter.

He stuck out a hand and smiled the bandage rising on his face. "Hey Dexter. I'm Samantha's brother, Peter. Glad to meet you."

I gave him a limp wrist shake still confused to why he wouldn't punch me in the face.

"Nice to meet you. About the other day... I'm so sorry..."

He held up a hand and deflected my plea for forgiveness. "Don't worry about it. You didn't know. I haven't been kicked that hard since I took a guy's applesauce in prison," Peter said, with a grin.

Taken aback by his genuine smile and grace extended. I beat the shit out of him after all. Few people are that forgiving. Those kinds of people make me nervous.

"I know we didn't start on the right foot. Usually the beatings come later. Maybe we can make this family thing work," I said, with a grin.

He laughed. "I know Samantha never told you about me. That's not her fault. I'm kind of the joke of the family. Most of them pretend I don't exist. I did some stupid things and it bit me. It is what it is..."

"I can relate," my father said, now pushing the twins on the swings.

"I've been in jail for the last five years. I had everything going for me. Good job. Good money. Wife and kid's. I guess it wasn't enough. I made bad decisions and have to live with the consequences. Which includes the embarrassment for my family," Peter said.

"What did you do? I need to makes sure you're not a pervert or something. For your nephew's sake," I said, glancing at the twins.

"Not a pervert. No child molestation on my rap sheet. Check fraud, gambling, soliciting a prostitute, computer hacking, and operating a false corporation. Boring stuff."

I nodded my head listening to the list of offenses. "Well, good to hear nothing too serious. Wink. Wink."

"Those days gone. I was young caught up in it. Bored. Trying to find a way out of LeClaire. This place can be stifling. You know what I mean?"

"Yep. Been here my entire life. Everyone knows everybody's business. We're all trying to find ourselves. Still am," I said, with a smirk.

Waved my dad to stop pushing the twins in the swing. "I want you to meet someone."

My dad let the swing finish twins still laughing with joy. "This is my dad, George."

Peter and dad exchanged handshakes and smiled back at one another. "It must be great having grandkids," Peter said.

"Sure is. I met them for the first time a few days ago."

Peter raised his eyebrow. "Why's that?"

"I've been in prison for the last thirty years. I got out a couple weeks ago."

Peter smiled and shook his head. "Funny. I got out of the joint yesterday. I was in Leavenworth."

George stared down at the sand. "Wow. Me too..."

"I was in BLOCK A. You?"

"BLOCK D."

"That's why you don't look familiar."

"Yeah. Leavenworth is a big place."

They exchanged a couple more stories of life in prison. I went back to the twins and let the jailbirds chat more while I pushed them in the swings.

My dad yelled out. "Son. I'm gonna talk with Peter more on the bench," he said, pointing to a wooden bench under an Oak tree.

They talked for another ten minutes and a car pulled up at the side of the park.

Peter said, "My ride's here. Nice meeting you George and Dexter. Hope to see you again soon."

Peter waved and disappeared in a truck driven by Samantha. She didn't look in my direction.

# Chapter 27

The pungent smell of urine, blood, and adultery filled the smoky Crazy Eight Motel room. Peter paced the dirty yellow shag carpet itching his armpits covered in flannel. He twitched like a heroin addict while smoking a cigarette.

"Why you so nervous?" George asked, sitting on the brown and yellow patterned comforter in the vintage room.

"I need a little time to let this all sink in. Wasn't ready to get back in the game so soon. Imagined a little hiatus between jobs, that's all," Peter said, taking a drag on his unfiltered Camel cigarette.

George leaned on his side on the bed and searched an end table for a pen and paper. He overlooked the pad sitting on the top of the table. "We need a better plan. Dexter is clueless and knows nothing is going on. At least I think. But the Buffone family are a problem. They want blood and will take it out of my ass if we don't do something fast."

Peter nodded in agreement and peeked out of the dusty gold curtains to the parking lot. "I'm not sure George. These Italian's are not messing around and want you dead bad. I felt safer in prison. The outside is like being naked."

George turned red and got in the face of Peter gripping his collar. "Listen. I don't give a shit of how you feel. You need to stop being a pussy. In Leavenworth we had a deal. I keep you alive from the Red Dragons and you help me with the Buffone's when we got out. I put my neck on the line and insured those racist assholes didn't hurt you. Now it's your turn to scratch my back."

The Red Dragons were a white supremacist group who didn't like Peter because he was black. George ran a small bartering business on the inside keeping different warring groups happy. He produced a DVD player smuggled in through the laundry service which made the Red Dragons forget about Peter for a while. By the time they wanted to hurt Peter he was released.

Peter was an adopted brother of Samantha and never fit small town life in LeClaire. He grew up with a single mom in Detroit who gave him up after getting locked up for prostitution. He acted out trying to find the love of a father he never knew. Crime was a search for love.

"Okay. You don't need to call me names. I'll keep my word. But, when this shit's done with the Buffone's, I'm out. I gotta get my shit together," Peter said, smashing the cigarette in a glass ashtray.

George sat down at a small table and scribbled on the notepad. He looked up deep in thought and then wrote more. Peter hovered over his shoulder.

He held up the paper with a list of names on it. Each name underlined and connected with lines to one another. "Here's the people we need to kill," George said, pointing with the pen.

Peter fiddled with his shirt pocket and lit another cigarette. He held up the paper in one hand and cigarette in the other, "Who are these people?" he asked.

George pointed at the paper like explaining a dysfunctional family tree. Peter ripped it out of his hands and plopped back on the bed puffing his cigarette.

"Who's Joe?"

"He's a used car salesman at Buffone Used Cars."

"Elizabeth?"

"Wife of the Chief of Police."

"Larry?"

"The Chief."

Peter circled a name on the Crazy Eight Motel stationary and held it up to George. "Really?"

"Yeah, that one's complicated. But, he knows too much."

"He's your only family."

George enacted Dr. Jekyll and Mr. Hyde and switched from calm and melancholy to volcanic.

He slammed his fist on the table. A paper cup of coffee spilled and dripped off the side onto the yellow shag carpet. "You know what? I don't give a shit about Dexter. Family sticks with you through thick and thin. They left me in that hell hole for thirty years. Not one visit. One call. No letters. Nothing. Screw them..." George said, leaning back in a black leather chair, a tear welling up in his eye.

Peter put up his hands in innocence, "All right. A deal is a deal. You can sort out the family drama on your own," he said, wadding the list of names in his pocket. "Let's get out of this roach motel before we catch something."

A knock at the door.

"You guys ready?" a deep voice called out.

# Chapter 28

George and Peter stepped into a LeClaire Missouri police cruiser. A wide man, with four stars on his lapel, and LPD issued uniform turned the wheel saying little. He peeked out the window and took a sip from a metal coffee mug.

"The Buffone's are breathing down my neck. They're losing patience. We need to get them their money or something front page worthy in the LeClaire Gazette is going down."

Peter smirked at George and elbowed him in the side. He leaned over and whispered something in his ear.

"What you two love birds giggling about?" the officer said, bending the rearview mirror down for a better angle.

"Nothing. Peter told me a funny joke. You want to hear it?" George asked.

"Knock knock."

"Who's there?"

"Dead-Chief."

"Dead-Chief who?"

"I know a dead Chief," George said, with an evil grin.

The Chief placed the coffee mug in a holder, "Hilarious old man," he said, shifting in his seat.

George's face turned from grins to intense focus as a silver blade slid from under his Members Only jacket. He raised the knife over the back of the Chief of Police's neck. He grimaced in the rearview mirror making his last facial expression on earth.

"I told you... I know a dead-Chief," George said.

The blade pierced through the back of his neck and out the front. Blood splattered over the seats and on their faces. The Chief made no sounds and fell to the right; dead.

Peter reached from the backseat to grab the steering wheel keeping the car on the road. He crawled over the seat and hit the brakes while sitting on the bloody Chief. The cruiser veered to a stop on a side gravel road.

Peter snapped a picture on his cell phone off the bloodied and slumped over Chief. He placed the Chief's hat back on his bloody head. Peter sent the attached picture in a text to someone in his contacts.

"Good work, kid. That was easier than I expected," George said.

Peter shoved the dead body against the passenger seat while George stayed in the back of the police cruiser. They drove in the dark to an abandoned home in the country.

Peter parked the cruiser. George pulled out a red gas tank they had bought at a gas station and doused the car with fuel. He threw a match on the soaked vehicle and sat back to watch it burn.

Peter gave him a high five as he lit up a cigarette. "One down. A few to go."

George and Peter hitchhiked back to the center of LeClaire. Peter went back to his mother's and George showed up on Dexter's porch and knocked on the door.

He acted like nothing happened.

"You have a good time with Peter?" Dexter asked.

"Great time! Visited an old friend."

# Chapter 29

We stood in the doorway and cold air punched us in the face. I tapped my watch, "Where you been old man? It's way too late to be hanging out with friends," I said, tongue in cheek.

George didn't look me in the eye and rushed past me. "I was with Peter and then met up with Larry Saxon, an old high school friend. I've not seen him since graduation. One of the few still in LeClaire from class of 1970."

I held up a plate from the dining room table and waved it toward dad. "You want me to warm a plate? You hungry...?"

My father wandered in and out of the room not sure whether to sit or stand. He fidgeted with a pant pocket and scratched his head like looking for lost keys.

"I'm fine. I ate dinner with Peter- I mean Larry," he said, taking off his tennis shoes, and placing them at the front door.

"You sure? I made macaroni and cheese with

bacon. My go-to-meal when Samantha gone," I said, taking out a fork from the drawer.

I raised my head up and smelled the air. "You smell gas?"

"Oh, yeah. I spilled gas on my hands when helping Larry fill his car. I'll go shower up."

"It's fine. You sure you don't want to taste down home cooking?"

I stared at the plate of noodles and bacon shrapnel thinking about Samantha. She only let me make "macaroni bacon surprise" when she had dinner with a girlfriend. The kid's liked it.

My father waved his hand and turned his back to head down the hall. "I will shower and hit the hay. I'm too tired to be out this late."

"Okay... I'm glad you got to see friends. I'll see you in the morning. Sleep good," I said, covering the macaroni surprise with foil and placing in the fridge.

I rocked in the recliner and thought about my father's strange behavior. He seemed nervous and uneasy. My phone rang on a side table. I looked at the caller ID: NO ID. Ignored the call as is my policy with any "NO ID."

I expected Samantha to call.

She never did.

# Chapter 30

Early the next morning, I leapt from sleep to my phone ringing in my ear. Samantha sounded panicked on the other end of the line. I tried to get her to slow down her speech. "What happened?"

She huffed and puffed like she ran from the other room. "I went into Peter's room this morning..."

"Tell me what happened sweetie?" I said, in a calm voice.

"I went into his room and..."

"And what?"

"Peter's dead."

I felt the room spin and get loud as I sat up in the bed. It recalled the last time someone called me because of a death. Lisa and Spencer.

"Tell me what happened?"

"I don't know..." Samantha said, weeping and trying to catch her breath.

"Where's your mother and the twins, Lisa?"

"Still asleep. They know nothing. What do I do, Dex? Tell me..."

"I'm coming over right now. Call no one yet, and make sure your mother, and the kid's don't see Peter."

I woke up my father sleeping in the guest room. "Dad, something happened to Peter. I need to leave and see what's going on."

My father rubbed his eyes and spoke in a hoarse voice, "What happened, Peter?"

"I don't know everything yet."

"Can I help?"

"No, just get rest, and we'll catch up later."

"Okay, son."

I sped down highway 70 in the Ford F-150 breaking most speed limits. A sense of fear washed over me thinking about Samantha and what Peter might be caught up with.

I arrived at the small ranch home and tapped on the screen door on the porch. Samantha peered around the door looking across the yard like someone might jump us. "Come in," she said, with a soft whisper.

"You okay?"

She waved me in and walked me to a back bedroom where Peter was. I stood over a red mound of body and blankets. I pulled back the red blanket off his cold body. A single bullet hole greeted me through the middle of his forehead. His eyes frozen open.

I took a second look and put the blanket over him again. I hugged Samantha and told her I was sorry about her brother.

"Who did this? Why, Dex, why?"

I embraced Sam and rubbed her back and whispered, "I don't know. But, we will find out, and make this right."

"Do we need to call the police?"

"Yes, that's the right thing to do. I want no one to think anything suspicious."

"We're not in trouble, are we?"

"Not unless you did this," I said, with a giggle.

Samantha pulled back and gave me a wicked stare, "No time for jokes."

"Did you hear any strange noises this morning or last night?"

"I didn't hear Peter come home last night. He said he would visit a friend and wouldn't be back until late. I went to bed at 9, and he was gone. I don't know when this could've happened."

Samantha trembled with tears. She gripped me tighter and dug her nails in me. "Did someone come in the house and kill Peter last night? I don't want psychopaths coming into my home where my babies sleep. Can't live like this Dexter..." Samantha said.

Didn't know what to say at this point. I tried to piece together all that happened in the last few days and the roads curved. My father being kidnapped and threatened. Peter coming into the picture, now gone. "I don't know, sweetie. Whoever did this must've known Peter. They put him back in his bed after killing him, or snuck in the house, and shot him. Did you see any sign of a break in?"

She shook her head. "I checked all the doors, and they were locked all night."

I could hear the twins cry in another room. "You get the boys and I'll call the police."

Samantha's mother poked her head in the room. "What's going on in here?"

I looked at Samantha and she looked back at me. Peter was still under the blanket.

# Chapter 31

The heavy-set coroner crouched over the body of Peter and snapped pictures with a Canon digital camera. He moved around the room taking different angled shots like a model photo shoot. Samantha's mother sat curled on the couch while LeClaire PD questioned her.

A skinny officer made small talk in the corner of the living room about the T-Bones minor league baseball team and the extra cool weather we were having for spring in Missouri.

I recognized the officer. "Where's your flat top sidekick?" I said, making a gesture above my head. The officer stared at the floor like he'd lost a contact lens. He mumbled incoherent words over his notepad. "I don't know. He called in sick today. First time in five years."

"You going to be okay without your partner in crime? You seem on edge."

He didn't answer and looked to the side of the room having no intentions of locking eyes. The voices and talking ramped up echoing off the hard-wood floors. Men and women rushed in and out of the house investigating forced entry, dusting for fingerprints, and some standing around wasting taxpayer dollars.

John barreled into the house, Cherry Coke in hand, and scanned the room. "Good Lord. You having a party and not tell me?"

"Peter's dead."

I could see the air leave the body of John as embarrassment set in from his crude comment. "Peter, as in Samantha's brother?" he mouthed the words, "Really?"

I nodded and took off my John Deere hat and placed it on a hook. "Happened sometime last night. Found him this morning in his bed with a bullet through the forehead."

"Damn. Is the rest of the family safe? Sam, the twins, stepdaughter?"

"Strange part. She didn't hear a thing in the night. I think someone killed him and snuck him back into his bed in the night."

I waved John into a quiet back bedroom away from the noise and chaos. "It's time. People are dying left and right in this town. I think the Buf-fone family is behind this and we need to act now."

John put up his hands in resistance, "I don't know Dex," pulling out a phone, "check the front page of the LeClaire Gazette. Made national news."

I scrolled the article on the phone and looked back at John. "Oh shit. The Police of Chief got murdered? Body found burned in a field."

John looked as though he was thinking on a hard math equation. A bead of sweat formed on his pudgy forehead, "There's stuff going down in LeClaire that might be beyond our pay grade. I'm not comfortable mixing it up in these circles."

I leaned into John and our bellies touched (his being like Jell-O). John's warm breath splashed my face. "Listen, LeClaire is our city and we're called to protect her. Your family, my family, and our memories tied up in this place. I will not let sick bastards kill everyone why we sit back and let our incompetent police force share fart jokes at crimes scenes. My dad needs our help. Our community needs protection. That's the least we can do."

John is the rational and logical one. He needs time to consider next moves. Resistance is normal in the beginning for any job. I'm the cowboy. The OCD one, passionate, let's get er' done mentality. It makes for a balanced team.

John put out a hand for a fist bump. "All right, I trust you, Dex. Let's save LeClaire."

I walked over to a police officer and handed him a wad of cash, "Here's the deal. I need my family safe. Can you put them up at the Holiday Inn until things calm down? Tell them I'll catch up with them later."

The police officer looked stunned, smiled, and

then relented by shaking his head in agreement. "I'll take care of your family, sir. No problem."

"Tell your partner to feel better."

"Will do."

John and I drove back to the barn and worked out a plan.

# Chapter 32

I slid the barn door open and walked into the fresh smell of spring rain and mildew. The barn not the best place for serious bad guy work, but has been useful for keeping LeClaire safe.

I turned the whiteboard toward John and paced around the room. The names of dead people, suspects, events, and folks needing questioning, written across the front. Chief of Police dead. Peter dead. Guy in the Camaro. Buffone family. Elizabeth (wife of Chief). Brick through window. Graffiti in bedroom. Dad (George).

I wrote a new name on the board... LPD officer. "Who's that?" John asked.

I circled the name and gripped my chin pretending to look smart and in deep thought. "I had a random conversation with an officer at Sam's mother's house. He mentioned his partner didn't come to work today. Called in sick. First time in many years."

"So what? People get sick all the time. That doesn't sound like much of a clue."

"Maybe. But the last two times cops showed up to my house, a flat-topped officer was in tow. Peter gets killed, and he's a no-show. Coincidence? Maybe, maybe not?"

John scrolled a computer mouse and didn't look up from his desk monitor, "I don't see the connection, Dex? People get sick and take days off. I think you might stretch it connecting the flat-top guy with the murder of Peter. No?"

I rippled my fingers against the board and stared through the names. I kept looking as if they would speak and give the truth, "Think about it. LeClaire is not a big city and the pay for public service is pathetic. Many LPD take second jobs like security at Spunky's to make ends meet. Taking days off is not an option unless you're bleeding out of your eyeballs. Flattop is either sick, or hiding something."

John peeked up from the computer and contemplated my theory. He turned to the left in his swivel chair and leaned back, "I see your logic, maybe? I think it's a giant leap from sick day to murderer."

"I'm not 100% flat top murdered Peter. But, he could easily be involved. I'm keeping his name on the list and not ruling him out until I see a doctor's note."

John walked over to the white board, picked up a marker, and circled Buffone Family.

"I think this is where the blood trail leads. I don't know if they're connected to Peter's death. But, why they want a thirty-year-old debt paid, and why they want your dad dead, makes little sense. They seem like irrational thugs. If anyone would kill Peter to make a point, it would be the Italian's. How's your dad?"

"I think he's okay. He came home late after seeing a friend and seemed a little weird. I'm sure he didn't expect to be caught in all the drama. Prison easy compared to this nonsense."

"No doubt..." John waved me over to the computer, "Come and see this," he said, pointing at the LCD monitor.

I leaned over John's shoulder and looked at lines racing across the screen like a heart monitor. "Oh, this again. How's the experiment going?"

John is always looking for the most humane ways to kill people. It's his way of easing his conscious (in our line of work). "I'm close to getting the right voltage for shutting down the brain of a victim. It's painless. Check this out..."

John walked to a cage where a mouse scurried around wires coming out of its small head. He jogged back to his computer and punched in a few commands. He glanced back at the mouse to see its response.

Nothing.

He glided back to the cage, fiddled with wires, and tried it again.

Nothing.

"Not working?" I asked.

John turned red and slammed his fist on the computer desk. "Dammit. I had this thing working yesterday."

I massaged his shoulder. "Keep working at it big fella. It'll come around. It always does."

I left John to play with his mice and headed back into the house. I needed sleep for a funeral was taking place in the morning.

# Chapter 33

The hairspray in Samantha's hair caused me to sneeze as she leaned into my side. A pastor's voice droned on in the distance reminding the congregation of hope, salvation, and eternity. I wiped her tears with a tissue.

Peter came into the family when he was five. His mother gave him up after living in the drug-infested projects of Detroit with no hope or future. Samantha's parents wanted another child after losing their son to cancer when he was six.

Peter never fit in being African America in a white family. Teased and got all the stares living in a LeClaire community with little diversity.

Samantha, the older sister by seven years, took on the role of mother hen. She felt responsible for protecting Peter from bullies. Samantha learned to fight at a young age when other kid's would call Peter nigger and comment on his different hair.

I love her toughness.

I peeked around the funeral audience seeing

who was in attendance. The usual aunts, uncles, cousins, and others who got out of LeClaire. Small town life can feel claustrophobic. But when someone dies, they pull together. It's like everyone dies for a moment.

I craned my neck and caught a well-dressed man standing in the back of the last row of chairs. He looked at his watch as if being late for an appointment. His black hair slicked and suit meticulously pressed. He adjusted his necktie and looked around the gathering.

In the last couple days my "bad guy alert" was in full force. With the latest killings of Peter, and the Chief, and roughing up of my dad, I was jumpy. I whispered in Samantha's ear, "Take a second and look at the man at your 3 o'clock." She wiped her nose and glanced in that direction trying not to be obvious.

"The guy in the nice suit? He looks Italian. You know him?"

"Nope, but he looks out of place," I said, looking back to the pastor finishing his message.

"He's making me nervous."

"I agree."

The last funeral I attended was Lisa's and Spencer's two years ago. I didn't handle that one well either. I bolted and had a drink at O'Malley's in the middle of the ceremony. John tried to rescue me from my introversion and the inability to handle pain of that magnitude. I also ran into a guy in a suit and things didn't go well. For the man in the suit that is.

The pastor winded down his message and gave the typical Amen. People were sobbing and mingling with casual chit chat. The weight of death and awkwardness ran through the crowd. Not sure what to say to the cousin you haven't seen in fifteen years. I kept my eye on the mystery man at the back of the lawn.

We mingled and chatted with relatives and distant cousin from other states. I can't tell you most of their names as Samantha's family is three times the size of mine. Old Testament times big. I gave my usual nod when she says, "You remember so and so..."

"Oh yeah that guy..." lying through my teeth.

I felt a tap on my shoulder. The man in the nice suit was standing center stage. I held a hand up to Samantha. "I'll be right back."

The mystery man held out a hand covered in gold bracelets and rings. I stared at his hand like it was a foreign object, "Dexter, is it?" he asked.

"Yes," I said with hesitation, "Do I know you?"

"Well, not really. But, you know my brother, Joe."

I snickered, "Joe... There's a thousand Joe's in LeClaire?"

The man in the suit turned from a pleasant smile to sure he wanted to punch me in the throat, "Joe Buffone... it's a family name."

"I'm sorry, man. Didn't mean to offend you. Don't know a Joe."

He adjusted his red tie and played with his gold cuff links before responding, "You and another gentlemen visited him at our families' dealership a couple weeks ago."

I placed my hand on the inside of my coat to make sure my pistol holstered. The Italian was not here to drop off flowers and best wishes.

"Not sure what you're talking about? I have a great vehicle and no need for a new one. No need to visit a dealership as you insist," I said, with a smile.

"You don't recall visiting Buffone Used Cars and roughing up my brother?"

I put up my hands in the sign of innocence and redness filled my Irish face, "There's that name again. Will plead the fifth on this one. I recall no visits to a dealership or run-ins with... Joe... is it?"

He gripped my shoulder and swung me around behind a tree shielding me from the grieving crowds. Slammed me against the tree and I could feel bark stabbing me in the back. He pressed his forearm into my neck.

"Listen, paison. I'm tired of your games. My family doesn't take kindly to punks roughing up our brothers. We don't forget these kinds of things. Oh yeah, and a friendly reminder, we still need our money, or your pops is done."

I was done negotiating. Thinking about my father and the deaths in LeClaire. Needed this to end. I'd be damned if this greasy Italian would ruin a funeral.

Kneed the Italian in the baby maker, spun him around, and I slammed him against the tree. Could hear his suit ripping against the rough bark.

"It looks like I'm the negotiator now. I too have a family who don't like being fucked with. Let's make this easy. I know you know a lot about holding debts and grudges, like the one with my father," I said, yanking out my pistol from inside my jacket, and jamming it into his cheek. Drool dripped onto the grass and my shoes. "You will forget about his debts and move on. If not, this gun will explode your brains all over this tree, and we will have your funeral today."

The Italian tried to speak with the gun pushed up his lip. "Easy... paison. I came here to scare you a little. We're good. No harm, no foul. Let's forget this ever happened."

I pressed harder with my forearm in his neck and the pressure of the gun clanked his tooth. "Tell the Buffone's leave my family alone. If not, this will get a lot uglier."

I released him from the tree and jammed my gun back into my pants. "Excuse me, I have a funeral to attend."

I walked back to Samantha and the rest of the

family. "Everything okay? You find the guy in the suit?" Samantha asked.

"Just an old family friend. He had to leave."

# Chapter 34

I'd hoped the funeral would cover a multitude of sins in the last couple of days. No luck. The funeral was not oiling the love grease between Samantha and I.

Instead... I sipped Jack and Coke's at O'Malley's with John.

I stirred a small red straw and poured out my heart to John. That's what happens when I get lubricated with alcohol, "I'm not sure we will make it, man."

John punched me in the arm almost spilling my drink and peanuts, "Don't say that Dex. There's a lot going on she needs time to sort it out. A few weeks ago she didn't even know you had a father. Now people want to kill him. That's a lot."

"True, but things aren't looking good. I was sure the funeral would do wonders," I said, chewing on a piece of ice.

John was the positive one of the team. He always tried to find the silver living, the full part of the cup, and all the other cliches of positive thinking. It had more to do with not having many relationships to base any advice on. "Give her a few days. Let the death of her brother set in, and she'll come around. You guys will be fine, a world without Dexter and Samantha is a sad place."

Smirked at John, "How long you been waiting to share that line?"

"Thought of it on the way over, good right?"

I smiled and felt a little better with John's counsel, "Want to hear something funny?" I asked.

"Always."

"One of the Italian's came to the funeral."

John paused, took a sip of his Whiskey Sour, and opened his eyes wide. "What? The Buffone brothers?"

"Sure, whatever the hell their names are."

"What did he say?"

I slammed my drink on the wooden bar top and stood like a preacher ready to fire up the congregation. "That greasy asshole had the audacity to threaten me and my family. He wanted money for dad, and confronted us, about beating the shit out of his brother."

"Dude at the dealership?"

"Yep, that dude. Apparently, the Italian's are not happy with us" I said, slurping my drink.

The room spun as the alcohol did its work, "What did you say? You're slurring your words," John said.

"Oh, Johnny boy. My dear friend John, I did a bad thing, a terrible thing. I threw that slimy Italian against a tree, pulled a gun, and told him: kiss my ass."

"You did what?"

"Everything is true except the ass part. I told him we aren't paying though."

John called the bartender over and sucked down another Whiskey, "I don't know Dex. That might've been a bad idea. You might've pissed off the queen bee and the nest will be on attack mode."

"I don't know of any queen bees in LeClaire. But no one will hurt my family that's for damn sure."

I stood up to use the restroom and try to pee out my drunkenness. Leaned against the bathroom wall reading the advertisements for a country band playing at County Fair. A couple men laughed behind me.

I turned my head and glimpsed a skinny older man leaving the restroom. Zipped up and followed the men into the bar.

My eyes became blurry as I followed the men. It looked like my father but I wasn't certain. I stumbled to the table of an older man and two other dark haired guys.

"Hello son, meet my new friends."

# Chapter 35

Two men smoked cigarettes, drank bourbon, and dad sipped on root beer. He laid off the sauce after seeing its effects in early life. I tried to refocus my eyes with buzz in full force.

"Good to see you again Dexter," said a dark-haired man, in an immaculate suit sipping bourbon.

I squinted and focused on his wide nose, "Why are you here with my father?"

A man sitting next to him in a similar nice suit butt into the conversation and wrapped his arm around my dad, "Georgie-boy is our new friend. He's working with us to pay off his debts. You know like washing dishes when you can't pay your bill," he said, a waiter smirked at the next table placing glasses and dishes in a black tub.

I reached for the back of my pants and realized my gun was in the car. I felt a presence come up behind me. It was John, "Who are these guys?"

One man rose from the red leather booth and

reached to shake John's hand. He opened his jacket flap and flashed his gun, "We are friends of George. Having a friendly conversation. He's working for us now."

John chuckled, took a sip of his whiskey sour, and glanced at me, "That true Dex? These guys don't look like friends...."

"Not at all... I'm trying to figure out what the hell they're doing with my father. I was clear about the arrangement we made at the funeral," I said.

My buzz ramped up and my knees buckled and room continued to spin in concentric circles. The images of the two men, and my father, were swapping positions like a video game.

Dad reached for my hand resting on the table, "Son, these gentlemen are helping me out. I will do a couple jobs for them and they'll forgive my debts. They promised."

"You will trust these greasy Italians? These guys probably killed Peter and the Chief of LPD."

An Italian sipped a drink and ignored my threats, "Careful paison. Don't make accusations for things you know nothing about. You keep jawing and the old guy will visit the Big Meatball in the Sky."

"That's not happening now or ever," John said, taking another sip of his drink. He reached into his blazer pocket and fiddled around with its contents. He turned his back on the table and nodded me toward him. His gun strapped in a holster on the inside.

I leaned over the table and got in close looking around the empty bar and saying in a whisper, "Listen, we talked about this. You mess with my family and you mess with me."

I grabbed the man by the back of the head and slammed it on the tabletop. Liquid from the drinks shot up like fountains in Paris. John slammed the butt of his gun into the temple of the other Italian. I locked my arm around my father and dragged him out of the restaurant.

The men moaned in the middle of bourbon soaked table.

"What are you doing Dexter? This was not a good idea," my father said.

"I'm saving your life. These are bad people and you need not do them any favors."

In the parking lot my father gripped my drunken face by the chin, "This was a way out. I could do a couple small jobs, pay my debts, and move on with my life. You're fucking things up."

"I'm fucking things up? You getting Alzheimer's in your old age? Without me picking you up from prison where would you be? You seem to forget the death threats, the brick, Peter, the money? These Italian's are not messing around and someone will get killed. You, me, and our entire family. That's a risk you want to take?"

My father stepped back and released my chin.

He kicked up gravel from the parking lot floor, "Honestly, I don't know what I want anymore."

John, George, and I hopped in the F-150. We headed home on the dark highway. I stared in the rearview mirror as a car behind us flashed their brights. I raised a hand to shield from being blinded.

The car sped up and almost tapped my bumper.

# Chapter 36

The truck rattled going faster than its V-8 was capable. A black Mercedes tailed almost hitting my bumper as I sped faster. George and John looked ahead focused on the road ahead.

"Can you guys see who's behind us?" I asked, looking out the windshield and checking the mirrors.

"I don't know, but I see two dudes in suits and a shotgun. One is holding a gun out the passenger window," John said, glancing out the right window.

I pulled my gun from the glove box and placed it in John's lap, "Use this."

John didn't like shooting guns if possible. He was more into nonviolent ways of killing bad guys. This might be a situation where nonviolence is not an option. He stared at the gun and let it rest on his lap.

The sound of clanking metal pummeled the side of the truck.

Bang. Bang. Bang.

Bullets flew past the vehicle some filling the white paint with holes.

I swerved thinking this might keep bullets from entering the truck. The truck rocked and squealed along the empty highway.

"John, use the gun. It's no time to pull a Martin Luther King Jr. These guys want us dead. Or... I'll do it."

John held his flabby arm out of the truck and tried to squint and fire off a shot. The first shot flew ten feet over the roof of the Mercedes.

"You hit anything?" I asked.

"Way off."

The next shot grazed the hood of the car and it swerved and pulled back to center of the lane.

"Got 'em," John said, with a surprising grin.

I peeked at the mirror and could see their speed was not slowing and they were almost on top of my bumper. The car was much smaller than the truck and could almost fit under the bed.

A shot rang out and the back window popped and the glass shattered. Spiders of cracks around the hole made it impossible for me to see them any longer.

"Shit, I replaced this window. Everybody okay?" I asked.

My dad said nothing and sat frozen-like. I hit his leg, "You okay? Not saying much for a guy with bullets flying by his head. Why don't you lay down and cover your head? This didn't turn out well for you last time."

The wind from the broken window whistled into the truck and made it hard to hear anything. I gave John a stare, "Why you not shooting these assholes?"

John had forgotten his job and looked nervous maneuvering the gun to take another shot, "Get those bastards," I said.

John fired again hitting nothing.

I heard a crash and the passenger mirror flew off into the Missouri night bouncing along the highway, "That was close," I said, looking at my dad.

He still looked stoic.

Another pop. My dad looked over at me with a confused look and slumped over in the front seat. A pool of blood grew on his upper shoulder through his white polo shirt.

I shook him, "Dad, you okay? Dad... Dad..."

My father lay motionless bleeding on the front of the white leather seats in the truck. John took another shot and hit the front right tire of the Mercedes. It spun out, flipped over, and rolled a few times in the distant, kicking up dust and dirt.

I craned my neck to see out the driver window. Headlights and dust swirled on the gravel road next to the highway. I high-fived John, "Good shot big fella. Not so bad."

"I prefer other methods of killing, but it was okay," he said, with a sheepish grin.

John peeked from the extended cab and saw my father lying in a heap of silence and blood, "Is he okay?"

"They got him. I'm heading to the hospital right now."

I placed my hand on my father's still head and pleaded with God to let him live.

# Chapter 37

I sat slouched in a small chair next to the hospital bed listening to the beeps of machines, doctors, and nurses, speaking in codes and medical lingo. A tall, balding doctor walked into the room with a clipboard.

"Your father's lucky. He's not out of the woods. But he's stable, and that's what we want. The gunshot wound missed all major organs," he said, scribbling something on the clipboard.

Placed my hand on my father connected to a mask for oxygen and wires coming out of his veins. I caressed his cold and frail hand. Glanced up at the doctor, "Good to hear. I always thought kids weren't supposed to outlive their parents."

The doctor nodded in agreement and peeked at his clipboard, "I know this isn't a good time. But the police need to talk to you about the shooting. Can you speak to them now?"

"Yes, send them in."

My heart raced wondering how to explain all

that happened a few hours earlier. The doctor left the room and two officers came into the room.

"Mr. O'Kane?"

"Yes, that's what my mother called me."

One officer looked Hispanic, and the other sported a flat top. I thought to myself... Oh shit. The flat-topped officer again.

He caught my eye and mine his. He pointed at me, "I know you from somewhere. I visited your home a few days ago. You off Cherry Street, right?"

I smiled and looked at my father trying to ignore eye contact. "Yep, that's us. I wish it were under better circumstances."

The Hispanic officer looked annoyed by the banter and got back to point, "Anyway. We need to ask you a few questions about what happened tonight. Where were you coming from when the shooting happened?" he asked, holding a black notebook.

"O'Malley's Pub off 39 highway."

The officer lit up for a moment, "That's a great watering hole. Irish Nachos are awesome. What were you doing there?"

"What do you think?" I said, rolling my eyes, and thinking why the LPD are incompetent, and need people like John and I, to do their dirty work.

"I know you had a traumatic evening, sir. But please keep the attitude in check."

"I was having a drink with my friend John," I said, pointing to his pudgy body curled up on a couch and snoring, "... and my father," giving his hand a gentle squeeze.

"Do you know anyone that wants to harm you or your family?"

"That's what I want to know. I don't think so. I pay my bills and try to be a decent human."

"How did your father get injured?"

I stared at the floor and tried to replay the incident in my mind, "It's kind of blurry. But I remember a black car riding up on my truck and almost hitting the bumper. They fired on us and a bullet must've come through the back window. I don't know."

"So you were driving the vehicle?"

"Yes."

"Anyone else in the vehicle?"

I nodded toward fatty on the couch, "John was in the backseat when it happened."

The two officers looked at one another about to say something. They seemed to hold back, "I know this is a trying time for your family. But, I need to administer a breathalyzer test. I know you came from the bar and I need to check your blood alcohol level. Driving drunk is no joke in Missouri."

My heart pumped out of my chest knowing I was full of liquor. More than the allotted amount in the state of Missouri, or any place.

I hoped my buzz wore off in the last couple of hours. I blew into the device and waited for a miracle. It beeped, and the officers looked at the red digital numbers. They shook their heads.

"I'm sorry Mr. O'Kane. You're above the Missouri limit for alcohol. We will have to charge you with a DUI."

I slumped back in my chair and looked at my father still asleep, "Are you shitting me right now? My father almost dies. Two crazies try to kill me and my friend tonight, and you will arrest me for a DUI? Go to hell."

The officers smiled unmoved by my anger, "Sorry sir. The law is the law. We don't mean to be the bearer of bad news."

The flattop officer reached for his handcuffs and placed one on my wrist, "One more thing."

I threw up my hands in a truce, "What now?"

"You're the brother-in-law of Peter Libson, correct?"

"Yeah, so what?" I said, wincing as he administered the second cuff.

The Hispanic officer grabbed me by the collar and lifted me to my feet, "You're under arrest for the murder of Peter Libson. You have the right to..."

John rubbed his eyes open and examined the altercation, "What the hell's going on? Why you in cuffs Dex?"

The flat topped officer pointed at John and his face turned to a serious tone, "Stay out of this fatty and you won't get hurt."

John sat back down on the couch and pouted at the comment.

The officers threw me in the back of a police cruiser and took me down to the LeClaire Police Department.

This was getting interesting.

# Chapter 38

The ceiling fan spun in the small interrogator room at the police station. A bead of sweat dropped onto the metal table as the officers stared through my nervous body. I contemplated my story and knew there was nothing on me... except the DUI. I didn't know how to get out of this one, yet.

"Mr. O'Kane. We will be recording this conversation," one officer said, placing a small device in the center of the table.

He hit the record button and the two men leaned back in metal chairs crossing their arms. They cracked a half smile.

"Please state your name."

"Dexter O'Kane."

"Where do you live?"

"429 Cherry Street, LeClaire, Missouri."

"Thank you."

I nodded and felt tension rising in the center of my chest. The heat in the room made it hard to think and focus on my alibi. I didn't understand why it was so hot in the room. Maybe to squeeze the perpetrator as they say in cop shows. But, I didn't think these guys were that good.

"Where were you on the night of March 3rd?"

I scanned the sterile room walls painted white and a small glass window reflected my face behind the officers. A few weeks of facial hair stared back at me.

"I was alone at my house for part of the night and then went to O'Malley's bar with John... for a drink."

"Can someone vouch for your whereabouts?"

"I said John was with me at the bar."

"Anyone else?"

"Your mom."

An officer who hadn't pushed a donut away for some time didn't find my humor amusing. He scowled and then reverted to the task at hand.

"Mr. O'Kane, you are being questioned about a murder. I don't think mother jokes are appropriate right now."

I snickered and knew these men hadn't handled a murder case in their lives. LeClaire is not a bastion of darkness unless you count the serial killer I took down a couple years earlier, "You know this is bullshit, right? I'm no murderer. You know it, I know it, and multiple people can vouch for my innocence."

The second officer took a drink of bottled water

and wiped his tanned forehead, "We'll let a jury of your peers decide innocence. We need you to answer our questions and stop your little jokes."

I clasped my hands together and hovered my chin above the table, "Like I said, I was at home and went to O'Malley's. My father and wife can vouch for me. He was at home and I called my wife that night too."

"Where was your wife on the 3rd?"

"At her mother's. We kind of got in a fight."

"Did you know Peter Libson?"

"Of course I did, he was my brother-in-law. Brother of my wife, Samantha."

"The black kid?"

"Yes, the black kid. I'm not sure what race has to do with anything," I asked.

"Nothing. It's just you don't see many blacks in LeClaire."

"Peter was adopted."

The officers nodded like they discovered gold, "That makes sense."

An image of Samantha crying in my arms at the funeral popped in my head. I didn't want to be in this boiling room any longer. I wanted to be snuggled on the couch with Samantha pretending none of this ever happened.

"When was the last time you saw Peter?"

I placed a hand on the top of my head and stroked it through my hair, "Ugh, a few weeks back. He came and visited me after he got out of prison. I was with my dad and kids playing on the playground. That was the first time we met."

"Were any words exchanged at the park?"

"I don't know. Normal stuff, like how are you? How was prison? Didn't know my sister had a brother."

One of the officer's scribbled on a note pad and inspected the audio recording device, "That's the first time you met. At the park?"

"Yep. Our families have a history of not talking about convict relatives."

"Do you know of anyone that might've wanted to hurt Peter?"

I placed my head in the middle of hands and stared at the table. Didn't want to answer any more questions and needed my bed, "I barely knew Peter. Met him a couple times, exchanged a few words, and that's it. I ain't no killer."

A knock at the door and one officer opened the door to greet another officer in the hall. They whispered and looked back at me. He waved for the other officer to come over. I sat fanning my face trying to cool off.

An officer turned off the recorder, "Mr. O'Kane. You can leave now. Thank you for the time."

He unlocked my handcuffs, and I rubbed my wrists trying to get blood back into the joints, "That's it. You question me for murder and letting me go, just like that?"

The officers were silent.

Samantha greeted me in the hall. I took a brisk step and grabbed her in an embrace, "What are you doing here?"

"I bailed you out. They dropped the DUI charge and are letting you go."

"What? I'm confused."

"Who cares, you're free. Let's get out of here before they lock you up again."

I didn't want to let her go.

# Chapter 39

The sound of pool balls echoed off the cement walls in the dingy basement. Twirling smoke like a twister rose in the air as five men sat around a card table. They dealt cards to one another playing a game of Texas Hold-Em.

"Who are these guys?" a voice asked.

"The Irish guy and his fat friend?" another voice answered.

A small man with pock marks covering his wide face smiled and rubbed the side of his swollen cheek. His left eye also swollen like punched by a prize fighter.

"You mean the Irish guy who punched your lights out?" a voice asked, as laughter filled the room.

"These guys know too much. We need to end this tonight."

An overweight man held a meatball sandwich in his hands and munched on it like it was his last meal. He chewed and wiped his double chin with a napkin, "The old man still owes us money. I always get my money."

A high-pitched voice piped in, "Let it go pops. He's in the hospital and going to die. Can't we focus on another job?"

The large man set the meatball sandwich on a plate, wiped his cheek, and took a drink of red wine, "Let me tell you a story, son. A long time ago when my pants fit a little looser. George O'Kane took something from me. He took one of my most prized possessions."

"What did he take? Your sandwich?" a man said, looking around the room for a laugh.

Silence.

"I have made millions in LeClaire and built many assets. But this George O'Kane took one of the greatest assets any human can have in all the earth. Family. And family can't be replaced."

"Did he kill someone?"

He wiped the corner of his mouth removing a splotch of marinara sauce and then dabbed a tear coming from his eyes. He tried to speak, "Many years ago this coward came into the 1st Bank of LeClaire and robbed the place. Your uncle Joe was working security that day. He shot him in the face and ran off with the money. Joe died that day. And, a bit of me died that day. I told myself that if George ever got out of prison, the death of my brother avenged. That day is today."

A smaller man placed his hands on the green

velvet card table. He tapped a cigar on an ashtray, "Whoa... I never heard dat story about the family."

The Don called the men over from the pool table, "I need everyone to hear this. LeClaire is our city. We run this place. I'll be damned if some old man and his son will get away with murder. No one kills a Buffone and gets away with it. You hear me?"

The men in the room all nodded and cheered.

# Chapter 40

The quiet of the hospital interspersed with beeping of machines and moans for pain medication. George rolled to his side and took a sip of apple juice. He reached for the remote and turned on a rerun of Seinfeld.

A knock at the door and a nurse came in to give him pain medicine. The short blonde smiled and handed him a cup of pills, "On a scale of one to ten... how's your pain?"

"Nine. I got shot you know," George said, with a flirty grin.

"Take these and we'll get that pain down to a three in no time. Press this button if you need anything else," she said, handing him a white device attached to the bed.

"I hope. I'm getting too old for taking bullets in the back. Can I ask you a question?"

"Sure Mr. O'Kane, what is it?"

"How do you do this job? I mean, with all the

sick, and dying people. Don't you get sad some-times?"

"That's a great question. I'm not sure. Maybe having great patients like yourself and seeing peo-ple get better. It makes it all worth it. Truthfully, I try not to think about it much."

"I wonder if people ever get better. I mean, we can get medication, and feel better. But, at our core, do we ever change? Can people heal in the soul?"

"That is a deep question Mr. O'Kane. I think so. Whatever doesn't kill us strengthens us, right?"

George nodded in agreement and felt sleepy from the pills and morphine, "Thanks Nurse Rosie. I think I'll sleep now."

The cute nurse pulled a blanket over George, turned off the light, and left the room.

George laid in the bed, coming in and out of sleep, with the TV still playing in the background. The glow of the tube glinting in his unconscious eyes. A crack of the door shed light into the room, "Is that you Rosie?" George asked, the whites of his eyes fluttering. "I'm fine. I want to sleep now."

A body pranced across the room as the TV got louder with the sounds of laughter. He opened a closet looking for something specific on a shelf.

The masked man found a pillow and inched closer to George sleeping a few feet away. He placed it over the face of George and pressed down.

George wiggled like a fish on dry land. The sound of the TV grew louder. The masked man pulled a gun from his jacket and placed it over the pillow.

He continued to flop and flail trying to yell for help and cry out to the nurse. A movie played in his mind of Dexter, prison, his wife, and grand-kids. He yelled with no sound rising above the pillow and loud TV.

The hammer of the gun fell. Blood soaked into the pillow as the TV drowned out the gunshot and the cries for help.

A man took off his mask, jammed the gun under his jacket, and opened the door. He waved to Rosie on the way out. She smiled and thought nothing of it.

# Chapter 41

The cool breezes of the evening whipped through the yard as we sat on a swing on the porch. It felt like the early moments of a first date. I tried to apologize to Samantha hoping she'd forgive my stupid actions.

Moon big and stars in full sight. I wore my glasses at night because contacts became too dry in the Missouri winds. I caressed Samantha's hand and drank of her blue eyes, "I'm sorry for being a moron. My dad is a big deal. But we all have skeletons in our family closets. Can you forgive? Can we start over?"

Samantha took a couple beats to think through a response, "I know we've only known each other less than five years. Things moved fast after Lisa and Spencer died. Dating, marriage, two kids, stepdaughter, and not to mention saving LeClaire. But you need to trust me. You can't be scared to share hard stuff of the past."

The O'Kane's were runners. Not joggers, rather,

people who don't face conflict head on. In hopes the issue will go away. A father in prison doesn't disappear like the sun in the evening. It lingers.

I gently kissed Samantha's hand and caressed her face, "Every family is dysfunctional. It's just hard to admit when it's your own."

Samantha nodded in agreement, "Come on Dex. I had a brother in prison. That's not something you mention over coffee at Rudy's. It's embarrassing."

"Nothing like incarcerated family members to bring a happy family together," I said, with a wink.

My phone buzzed in my pocket. I jumped off the porch and took the call, "Yes, this is Dexter O'Kane."

A woman on the other line told me to come to the hospital. It was dad.

"Who was that?" Samantha asked.

"It was the hospital. They told me to come right away."

Samantha and I drove together. First time in a couple weeks.

# Chapter 42

The nurse station at LeClaire Memorial filled with police officers, fire service, and frantic looking doctors and medical staff. A tall doctor came over, "Are you Mr. O'Kane?"

"That's what they call my father. Don't make me feel old. Dexter is fine."

He pointed to a man in a suit on the left side of the nurse's station, "An officer from LPD would like to speak with you for a moment."

"I did this, what now? Where's my father?"

The doctor walked away and disappeared into a sea of people, "Hello Mr. O'Kane. I'm detective Roger Connelly and I work with LPD," a square jawed well-built man said, flashing a badge.

I peeked over his shoulder and tried to get a better look into my father's hospital room, "Detective? What does this have to do with my father? Can I speak to the doctor?"

The agent reached for my shoulder, "I'm sorry to inform you. Your father was murdered tonight."

I felt the room spin and the words in my ears jumbled and in slow motion. Samantha looked up at me, "Can you repeat? My father is in room 112 and getting better. He can't be dead."

"A nurse came into your father's room tonight and found a bullet wound in his face."

"How did this happen? Isn't their security in the hospital," I said, feeling my face get hot in anger.

"We are doing everything we can to figure out what happened. I'm sorry."

"Damn," I said, wanting to strangle a man who was laughing with an officer across the hall.

"Were you close?"

"It's complicated."

The detective handed me a card, "Please call if you have questions or any leads. We will work hard on this case."

I thanked the officer and Samantha joined me on a chair against a wall of rooms. She wrapped her arms around my shoulders and we sat in silence. She rubbed my back and I couldn't remember the last time she touched me.

"I'm so sorry, Dex. This is turning out to be a shitty day."

"No kidding. Damn."

The detective came over and knelt down and asked a couple more questions. "I don't mean to bother you again. Is there any reason someone might want to hurt your father?"

I knew in the back of my mind a million reasons

and people who wanted dad dead. Imagined the Buffone family sitting in a restaurant eating spaghetti and laughing about the whole thing.

"Don't think so. He's an old man. Who does this kind of thing?"

The detective scribbled on a pad, placed it into his long brown coat, and stuck out his hand, "We'll be in touch."

Samantha continued to rub my back and feelings of sadness turned to rage,

"What you thinking?"

"You know how I said tonight my family are runners. I'm not running anymore."

"What do you mean?"

"I'm not sure yet."

"Let's go home and get rest, sweetie."

I stood up, pulled my phone from a pocket, and called John. Held my hand over the receiver, "Hold on one second. Need to make a quick call," I said.

Walked over to a corner of the hospital floor away from the noise and people. "John. Get ready. We're going tonight."

I hung up the phone and pretended everything was fine.

"Who was that?" she asked.

"A hotel. I booked a room for you, your mother, and the kids for the night. I don't think the house will be safe."

Samantha agreed, and I needed to figure out next steps. I was done running.

# Chapter 43

J ohn and I went to the barn, and I opened a
cabinet full of guns, knives, and ammo. John
tinkered with a device in his hand and showed
it. "Here she is. Finished."

I examined a white square device which looked
like a police taser. Tapped on the case and looked
back at John in confusion, "What is it?"

"Remember the project with the mice?"

"The electronic brain fryer thing?"

John snatched the device back into his pudgy
hands and aimed it at the barn doors, "No, idiot.
This will revolutionize how bad guys are handled.
I'm tired of seeing law enforcement, and guys like
us, only have options to shoot and kill. This electromagnetic device can sever brain function in its
victim with the click of a button. You can set to kill
or just paralyze."

"It looks like a garage door opener."

John gave me a stare and set the garage door
opener on the desk, "We might need my door

opener if we're going after the Buffone's. What's the plan, boss?"

I jammed a gun in my holster and looked down the barrel of a rifle, "The Buffone's killed dad, probably Peter, and the Chief. We know the target."

"You 100% positive?" John asked.

John's last resort was violence and wanted to ensure we killed the right guys. I would be lying if I had not been wrong occasionally. Live and learn.

"The suits who tried to run us off the road the other night. Guy in the black Camaro who tried to kill us at Leavenworth. Used car salesman. These guys are all connected to the Buffone's. All signs point to the Italian's."

I spun in a swivel chair and took a deep breath. I rubbed a pistol like petting a puppy, "These guys must die."

A moment of clarity hit John and walked over to my chair and scratched his head, "Your dad is dead. He was going to pay his debts, or get killed. Well, he's dead, why cause more chaos? This sounds like unnecessary revenge by the Italian's."

"LeClaire is our town. The Buffone's will not sit back thinking they can destroy people. Bad guys will not have the last say in my city, right?"

"I'm all for justice, Dexter. But we need to think of our own skin, your family, my family."

I didn't listen to John's little speech and hated the Buffone's with a deep rage.

I loved dad more than I thought. That's why they must die.

# Chapter 44

It was twelve AM the street quiet and moon-light bounced off my truck. I peeked over to the passenger seat examining the tools of the trade. Pistol, mask, and ammo. The job quick and to the point. How I liked it.

I held up the business card of the Buffone Used Cars dealership. An address handwritten on the back. I double-checked to make sure I was at the right house. A little Google and Facebook research paid off.

I picked up the pistol, loaded in the ammo, and adjusting the black mask. The wool made the top of my head warm. I said the Lord's Prayer, empha-sizing the forgiveness part, and unlocked the truck door.

I pranced around the side of a white two story house, probably 70's. Only light coming from the back windows of the house. TV room.

I kneeled down under the window and could feel my heart beating with adrenaline. Itched the side of my head with a leather glove and felt a drip of sweat trickle down the side of my face. Rose and peered into the TV room looking for signs of life.

A dark-haired man sat with his woman snuggling on the couch watching an LCD flat screen over a fireplace. The coffee table in front of them covered with wine glasses, tortilla chips, and guacamole. My stomach rumbled with hunger pangs.

I dropped as the woman got up from the couch. She yanked on her flannel pajama pants, and smiled, as she walked by the man on the couch. He nodded and mouthed words to her.

I slid below the window, crawled left, and made it to a back screen door. I turned the knob to see if it was unlocked. No resistance and kept moving.

Paused before entering to make sure the time was right.

Took a deep breath.

I barreled into the TV room gun raised straight out. The man looked in my direction with wide eyes. He held up his hands and didn't say a word. I did not speak and aimed the pistol between his dark brown eyes. I put my finger over my mouth to signal not to talk.

A thunderstorm rolled in from the backyard. The sound of thunder popped and flashed lighting up the house.

"Please don't kill me. Take whatever you want," the man said.

I motioned for him not to talk, "I'll do all the

talking. You took something from me. Something I can never get back."

"I don't know if you're a customer. But, I will make it right. Come down to the lot tomorrow and we'll take care of you."

The sweat from the wool cap dripped in my eyes stinging it from the salt, "I said... I will do the talking. You have customers holding you up at gunpoint because of bad deals at the dealership? That's a thing?"

The conversation became causal, "You'd be surprised. Working with the public is the worst."

"I know... at Antique... shit. I'm not here to chit chat. Let's get back to business."

I pressed my index finger on the trigger and felt it nudge. I tried to keep my hand steady and shook because of the wool cap causing heat stroke.

"Family is everything. You took out my father, and now it's time for you to pay."

The man's hands trembled in the air and his bottom lip quivered. "Daddy?" said a small voice from behind the couch.

"Ben, go back to bed. Daddy is busy right now."

The boy ignored his plea and came and sat on his lap, "That man has a funny hat. I'm scared of the thunder. Can you tuck me in?"

I locked eyes on the boy no older than four years old. I thought about the twins and daughter back at the motel and how much I loved them.

"Please, Ben. Go find mommy in the other room. She'll tuck you in."

The boy cried and leaned into the arms of his father. He laid in his lap and buried his face in his leg as thunder crashed made my heart jump.

I backed up toward the door. Couldn't do it.

"I'll see you again."

Ran to the truck and ripped off my mask as the heat was making my stomach hurt. Sat in the truck, rain bouncing off the hood.

John called, "Is it done?" he asked.

"No, I didn't have a chance."

# Chapter 45

A TV flashed light playing Law and Order reruns and I couldn't focus with the noise. Samantha sat propped on a twin bed flipping through her phone and daughter asleep. I laid on the other twin bed pretending to watch TV. The boys snored in their matching pack and plays. Mother-in-law slept on a pullout couch across the room.

The hotels in LeClaire not known for their four-star accommodations like in Kansas City or New York. I changed the channel and stared at the screen not focused on an infomercial for a cutting device, "You okay?" I asked.

Samantha rolled her eyes like I asked a stupid question, "I'm great. Living the dream."

"You feel safe?"

"Depends how you define safe. If you mean safe right this moment, yes. If you mean safe, in the ultimate sense, not so much."

I tossed my John Deere hat on a side table and

took a sip of Coke, "John and I are working on a plan. Everything will be back to normal soon."

"My version and your version of normal are not the same. Here you go again taking matters into your own hands. Who do you think you are? Let the police handle it."

I could feel the tension in the room as the AC kicked on. I spoke louder, "I'm not trying to be a hero. We know who killed your brother and my father. The police have found no suspects for the Chief, Peter, or pops. Shouldn't we do something?"

"How'd you figure that out? I know John didn't make the connections. He's too busy building gadgets in his basement."

I smiled and flipped to another channel. "True. I'm the muscle and strategist and he's the brains, sometimes. Change that, he's the mad scientist."

"I know you're good at finding bad guys, Dex. I get scared. Antique Adventures is your passion and you're good at that too. And, I have no fear of you getting a bullet in the head, when searching for rusty gold."

I jumped from my bed and slid in next to her on the twin, "You know you married a crazy man, right? Remember how all this started? You hired me to find a serial killer who slaughtered your family members. This is what we signed up for."

"Can this be the last job?"

I paused and knew what Samantha wanted me to say. Couldn't say it... yet. Loved Samantha with a ferocious love and would do anything to make her happy. But this justice thing, whatever this thing is, got into me.

"How's your heart? You still like me?"

"You didn't answer the question."

"Yes, we can talk later about the last job."

"No, give me your word now," Samantha said, holding out a pinky finger, "Pinky swear."

I stared into her eyes and smiled knowing how much she made me happy. I would say anything even if I was lying, "Pinky swear."

Samantha pushed a finger at the side of her mouth, "Do I still like you... Hmm... let me think for a moment."

"Not funny."

"I still like you. I want more stability and less drama. Antique Adventures is enough stress already."

I nodded in agreement. The antique business is not a steady monthly paycheck, "I know... I'm a cowboy looking for the next fight to win. This will be the last time, I promise, we pinky swore, right?"

"Dexter O'Kane... I know you too well. I'm not dumb. This will not be the last ride at the rodeo. You'll find something to get yourself into trouble."

I smiled, "Maybe knitting, sounds like that's becoming popular again. At least it's not dangerous."

There was a knock on the door, "Room service" a man's voice called out.

I leapt from the bed, pulled out my wallet, and paid the man. Nothing like greasy chicken fingers, pizza, and French fries, to end a stressful day.

"I'm sure the fine food at the Crazy Eight Motel won't give us diarrhea," Samantha said, biting into a French fry.

For a moment things felt peaceful and normal. I knew this would not last long, as someone needed to die, and die soon. Thought about being at the Buffone brother's house and not pulling the trigger. I glanced at my sleeping kids and knew wasn't an option.

But promises are often broken.

# Chapter 46

John and I sat across from one another in Ruby's Cafe eating eggs, bacon, and the best cinnamon rolls, in Missouri. I sipped coffee wincing from the heat.

"I'm at a loss." Probing John to give answers to the killings.

John wiped his pudgy cheek dripping with flakes of sugar from the cinnamon roll. He smiled with his normal optimism, "We'll figure it out. We need to cut the head off the snake."

"Explain."

"If we take down the boss all the other pieces will fall. We need to find the right Italian."

Slammed my hand on the sticky table our plates jumped up in sync, "Dammit, John. I know you're Mr. Positive and think everything will just work out. Stood in the living room of a man who most likely killed Peter and my dad, or at least was part of the plot. Didn't pull the trigger. Maybe we need to cut up the snake into pieces before we get the head. We may not get a chance like that again."

John sipped his coffee ignoring my pleas and watched a woman walk into the diner. He gave her a second glance like someone he knew. He whispered to me, "Is that Elizabeth?"

"Elizabeth... who?"

"The widow of the Chief of Police?"

"It is."

A tall slender woman wearing a tight skirt who worked out stood at the edge of our table. Her eyes looked tired like any woman who had lost a husband.

She poked my shoulder, "You Samantha's husband?"

I examined my shoulder in shock of her aggressiveness, "Yes ma'am."

"Heard about you guys."

I grinned and held a piece of bacon at the corner of my mouth, "Depends what you heard. Half of what people say isn't true," I said, she didn't look interested in small talk.

"Heard you get things done."

"I don't know what you heard, but, I'm just an antique dealer. You have an item you want me to appraise? I'll get you a fair price," I said, now intrigued by the conversation.

"Not antiques. I need help with a different project."

"Okay..."

Elizabeth pointed at the booth wanting to slide in and sit down.

I obliged.

She spoke in hushed tones trying not to alert the crowded diner, "My husband was killed by bad men. Specifically, a bad family."

John and I nodded and sipped our coffee feeling the mood of the breakfast getting serious, "I'm sorry about your loss. The Chief was a good man and did a lot of good for the people of LeClaire."

A tear formed in her eye and makeup ran. She reached across the table to the silver napkin holder and wiped her eye, "Thank you, but that's not all true. He got caught up in some bad stuff, with some bad people."

I put on my counselor hat and tried to be sensitive in my questioning, "Do you mind sharing? What kind of stuff and what kind of people?"

"Two years ago the LPD was under investigation for a couple bad seeds on the force. Accused of racial profiling and beating up unarmed kids in town. My husband was up for reelection and wanted to clean up the mess..." she said, and stared down at the table, and picked at a sugar packet.

I looked at John feeling the awkwardness of the crying woman, "Go ahead."

"He heard about the Buffone family and their involvement in LeClaire. He knew their businesses was a front for criminal activity. They could make things go away...if you know what I mean?"

We nodded in agreement.

The tears flooded her face, and I handed her another napkin, "He hired the Buffone's to make the problem go away. They killed a couple key witnesses and my husband was off the hook and got reelected. He promised never to do anything like this again."

"What happened after the trial?" I asked.

"The Buffone's held this against my husband and wouldn't leave him alone. It was a favor they used to manipulate and do more crime. They formed an alliance with LPD and things got ugly. The police were helping the Buffone's hide their crimes regularly. The department didn't care because everyone was getting paid well."

"So, not to be rude, what do you need from us? We're just antique collectors, not assassins."

She wiped her tears with the back of her hand, a gold bracelet dangling from her skinny wrist. Elizabeth's face became intense, "Let's cut the shit. I know what you can do. My husband told me. I want this family stopped. They took my husband and have made LeClaire their den of evil. The Buffone's need to be punished."

John and I both looked at one another knowing what needed to be done.

"I'll pay whatever it takes."

"Before we talk price. Do you know if the Buffone's have a regular hangout? Like a headquarters."

She dug into her red leather purse and pulled out a pen and business card. She scribbled a name and address on the card, "No problem. They spend time here."

I held the card out with my arms to let my eyes adjust. The old First Baptist Church on highway 24 is our next stop.

"Let's cut off the head of a snake," I said, winking at John.

# Chapter 47

At midnight we pulled the truck up around highway 36, hung a left on a dirt road, and crossed over to highway 24. The old First Baptist Church sat empty for almost thirty years at the edge of LeClaire in a town called Smalley. Rumor is preacher was getting tail from the secretary and the church never recovered. The building abandoned and inhabited by animals, and Italians.

I stared at the business card given by Elizabeth and scratched my head, "Why would the Buffone's hang out at this dump?"

"Maybe they feel guilty and think God will forgive them by meeting in a church," John said, sipping a Diet Cherry Coke.

I shut down the truck and parked about two hundred yards from the building on a side street. It didn't seem to matter as the church perched on a street with little activity. Smalley used to have a GM automobile plant that left with most of the industry. The jobs left and so did the people. The only other building an old grocery store from when the town had life.

John adjusted his extra-large bulletproof vest and checked the inside of his pistol. Loaded.

I rummaged through a large black duffel bag on the front bench of the truck and found more ammo. I locked them into my rifle and pulled a black mask halfway over my head.

The building looked quiet with only a single light hanging over a side door, "Straight up?" I asked John.

That was code for no bullshitting and rushing the front door with no time for the bad guys to respond. We've even caught evil on the toilet.

John gave a thumbs up, "They will not expect anything at this hour and in this ghost town."

We fist bumped, I said the Lord's Prayer, and locked the truck doors. We crept across the street and up a broken sidewalk toward the church. I don't know why we looked around the streets as the town was silent as an old film.

A glimmer of light shot through a crumbling stain glassed window of Jesus on the cross. I could see shadows moving around from inside the building. I waved John forward and pointed at the front door. I nodded knowing there were people inside the building as voices got louder with each step.

Laughter.

The front entrance was a rotting wooden door hanging to life. I examined holes in the door which appeared to be from bullets. I grabbed the gothic metal handle and pulled on it. The door gave way and needed WD40. I looked back at John for the go ahead.

I heard laughing getting louder in the distance.

We shuffled our feet, rifle in hand, pistols aimed, and hearts beating with fear. The room was not what I expected for an abandoned church. A wet bar to the left, high tables and chairs to the right, expensive art on the walls, and leather couches spread throughout the space.

I peeked through a second door window that led into the Great Room. A group of men sat in leather chairs drinking, eating, and laughing, not noticing that we were now standing in the center of the room.

"Put your hands in the air and don't even think about drawing weapons." I said, John scanning the room, with pistol aimed on half dozen men.

The laughter ended and most of the men's eyes opened wide. John aimed his pistol at the right side and I scanned my rifle to the middle and left. There were about six men we could see.

A heavy-set frumpy man in the middle of the group smiled as I pointed the rifle at the gold tooth in the center of his mouth, "Welcome friends. We thought you might make a visit. Would you like a drink?" he asked, waving to a man mixing drinks behind a bar.

Confused by the calmness of the man and

looked at John, he shrugged, "Shut the hell up and stop playing games. We didn't come here to have a drink. I don't drink with enemies. We came here to spill blood. Tonight all this shit ends."

The wide Italian was unfazed by my threats. He rolled a toothpick around in his mouth, "You don't think we know who you are, Dexter O'Kane. You're going to just waltz in here and kill us. That's now how the Buffone's work. We like to wine and dine our guests first and then kill them. Like we did your father."

My face throbbed hot, and I gripped the rifle tighter thinking I'd crush the wood, "Only monsters kill innocent old men."

"Looks can be deceiving. Your father was far from innocent. He took something of ours and needed to pay back his debts."

The Italian glanced to an upper level balcony where five more men stood with guns drawn.

My heart sank.

"Shit," I said, under my breath.

# Chapter 48

J ohn reached into a small pocket of his cargo pants and pulled out a small square device. He flipped a switch with his thumb and aimed at the men in the upper balcony of the church. From left to right the men crumbled to the floor guns splashing to the ground.

The Italian Don looked to the balcony with terror, "What the hell is this? How'd you do that?" he said, the other men chatting, and not paying attention to the situation.

"You're not the only one who thought ahead," I said, as the last man on the balcony slumped to the ground.

John waved the device at the Don and the other men, "A flip of a switch and you'll meet your Maker. You will stop whatever crime ring you have going in LeClaire. We don't like your types in our town."

The Don sucked on a cocktail and reached for a cigar, "My family has been in this town before you were born. What do you know about loyalty to a people? Sounds like Dexter wasn't loyal to his own father. You come here with loaded guns, and your death ray, and want to talk about crime. We know all about your little side business."

"You have your opinion and I have mine. I'm here to protect the innocent and good people of LeClaire. That means getting rid of scum like you, and your family. That's why I do this... save your lecture."

The Don smiled and pointed his cigar at the Jesus stained glass, "Don't lie Dexter, the Good Lord is watching you. You tell me...the antique shop is not a front, for the true, and real Dexter? I know you. You're a lot like me."

My hand trembled trying to keep the rifle steady aimed between his eyes. I knew on one level the Don was right. I was an elixir of contradictions not knowing why I do what I do. But aren't we all?

"I'm nothing like you. Different motivations for what I do. Not trying to build an Empire, like you."

"I used to say things like that. It helps soothe the conscious. I could use a guy like you, Dexter O'Kane. Now I'm short a few men," he said, looking to the balcony.

The room felt warm, and I blinked twice trying to shake sweat from my lids. Two images of the Don moved side to side in my vision.

"I'd rather burn in hell than partner with your sick ass family."

"Looks like your family is getting smaller, Dex-ter. Maybe you should reconsider being part of mine," the Don said, smiling at the men sitting at the right and left.

I thought of my dad, Peter, Samantha, the twins, and John who has been like family since birth. My hand twitched. I turned to the right and pulled the trigger exploding a perfect hole in the center of an Italian's forehead. He slumped to the right and blood raced to the floor.

Like dominoes, I made my way to the left, another dropped, another, and John laid two more down.

A smaller Italian threw up a card table to shield from my next victim, The Don. He grabbed him and disappeared through swinging doors in the back of the church. I waved John over and we tailed them into the darkness.

The kitchen smelled of mildew and furnished with steel counters, hanging pots, and commercial grade stoves. A kind of kitchen hungry Italians would need.

John covered my right, and I looked to the left. I heard a metal bowl crash to the ground, "Let's not make this any worse. There's no way out Buffone's. Your family is no longer welcome in LeClaire. Only two of us are going home tonight. You're not one of them," I said, winking at John.

I could hear the heavy breathing of an over-weight man in the back corner of the kitchen. He tried to catch his breath and speak, "You don't think those men were all family, do you? I'm smarter than I look, Dexter. When you think you've killed the Buffone's, they spread even stronger like a virus."

I peeked at John and he shrugged his shoulders, "We don't believe you. Don't think you're that smart. I call your bluff," I said, scanning the room trying to find the Don.

"Oh my little naïve paisano. I have more street smarts in my little pinky ring than your entire body. You know nothing of the evil I'm capable of, my Irish friend."

"Let's stop all the talking. I'm tired of conversation. You are hard to listen to."

Silence.

"You must be tired, too."

No response.

I pushed through a swinging door and peeked into the back of the kitchen thinking the Don would hide in there. A backdoor sat propped open. The sound of squealing tires, flashing red taillights, and kicked up gravel and dust filled the back parking lot.

A black Camaro disappeared into the dark early Missouri morning.

# Chapter 49

I pressed the gas on the F-150 and she revved beyond what the engine could handle. A warmth of adrenaline churned through my body like an oil rig working at full capacity. An image of The Don in my mind's eye forcing my foot harder on the pedal.

I had no idea where The Don might try to escape. Called Elizabeth.

She answered the phone with a groggy voice like it was the middle of the night, which it was.

"Dexter? Why are you calling me at two in the morning?"

"We found the Buffone's. Where else may they hang out?"

Elizabeth paused on the other line trying to shake the deep sleep from her bones, "Did you try the Baptist church?"

"Yes, we found a bunch of their thugs and killed some. But The Don escaped. I need to know where else they could be?" I asked, with a desperate tone feeling The Don slip away.

"There's an Italian restaurant called Serafino's on Main St. My husband told me it's a front for one of their businesses. The Buffone's eat there all the time. I'm not sure they'll be there at this time of night."

"It's worth a try."

I thanked her and hung up.

John didn't say a word and stared at his garage door opener in his lap. He smiled flipping the switch up and down, "Man... did you see this baby in action? Took those greasy Italians down like dominoes."

I smiled and kept thinking about The Don. I slapped John in the arm, "I knew it would work. Good timing, too," I said, in a stoic tone not wanting to chit-chat any longer.

"Where we headed?" John asked.

"Elizabeth said Serafino's on Main is where The Don might hang out."

"At this time of night?"

"That's what she said. It's worth a shot. We have little to go on right now. Like in a kidnapping, the first forty-eight hours are vital. The Italian needs to go down tonight."

John and I were like a married couple and could read each other's minds. He knew the times when I didn't want to talk. This was one of them. I was trying to think a few moves ahead.

I glanced up in the rearview mirror and a car was following close. No other cars were on the quiet highway as we made our way back into the center of LeClaire. The mystery car tapped my bumper.

"You see this asshole?" I asked, bending the rearview mirror down to get a better look.

The headlights flashed at me as if to tell me to pull over. When the lights faded, I could tell it was a Black Camaro.

I jammed the gas further into the floorboard feeling the bones in my foot turn and crack. "John, get a gun from the duffel bag. These guys want to play."

John loaded a pistol and peeked into the passenger mirror watching the car come close.

I heard the sound of gun fire all over the truck. It was not John, it was coming from the Black Camaro.

My last memory was gripping the wheel of the truck trying to keep it straight as a tire blew out. The truck swerved sideways a couple times, corrected, and veered into a light pole.

Our bodies lurched forward with tremendous force smashing faces into the dash.

Lights out.

# Chapter 50

I felt hands grabbing my shoulders and the heels of my boots dragging on the cement floor. My eyes filled with blood and John slumped over in the passenger seat moaning and groaning.

A voice said, "Hello, Dexter."

My eyes were open but everything was blurry. I couldn't speak.

"You thought I was dead. Remember when you tried to kill me at the prison?" a gravelly voice asked.

I felt a pit in my stomach and the movie of the prison playing in my mind. I remembered pulling a man out of a Black Camaro with a yellow hoodie.

The mystery man dragged me to the opposite side of the road away from the truck. My left eye became clear. He was wearing a yellow hoodie.

"I've been waiting for this day a long time," he said, with an evil chuckle. I could hear John cry out for help from the truck.

My head was not right and couldn't comprehend

what was going on and who this man was. It made little sense and seemed dream-like.

The man pushed my face into the gravel and I felt him playing with my hands. He tied both hands together behind my back with a plastic tie.

"My father always says, 'You let nothing get between family.' I try to live my life by this motto. How about you Dexter? Any mottos you live by?"

The side of my face throbbed and my eyes flashed in and out of clarity. Through a half cough I tried to speak, "What do you want? If you're gonna kill me, do it."

The hardness of the ground irritated the laceration on the side of my cheek. The mixture of dirt and blood stung the wound, "That's a great question. And this will all be over soon. Really... what it comes down to is blood. The bonds of family blood. And the blood pouring out of your cheeks. Just more of it," the mystery man said, with an evil laugh.

I heard feet crushing gravel and getting closer. John stumbled across the street with mangled face and holding his arm out and carrying a small device.

The man in the hoodie rose to his feet, "What is that? A garage door opener?"

John smiled and winced in pain as blood raced down his temple, "Nope. Garage door openers aren't deadly."

The man pulled a gun from the back of his blue

jeans and smiled at John, "I'm not sure what the hell that means but I wouldn't enter a fight with a garage door opener. Pistols are more reliable," he said, shaking the gun side to side.

John held out the device and detonated the switch. He looked up to see the result. The man in the hoodie looked around and wasn't sure what to do.

Nothing.

John tried again. Nothing. He hit the device against his leg, "Shit," John said.

"When my garage opener isn't working it's the batteries. Did you try replacing them?" he said, raising up the pistol and aimed between John's eyes.

"I'm sorry Dexter that you have to watch your friend die today."

John pressed the button one more time.

Nothing.

I laid on the ground next to the leg of the shooter. Did what any rational human would do when a gun pointed at a friend.

Bit him.

Felt the skin, tendons, and bones in my front teeth. He screamed, lowered the gun, and tried to shake me loose, "What the hell? You're biting me?" he said, as he kicked dirt in my face.

John pulled a pistol from his pants and aimed it at the hoodie-man, "Looks like we're holding all the cards now."

The man looked up in shock as John inched closer. "You won't shoot me. I'll put a bullet in your friends head before you even drop the hammer," he said, pointing the gun on top of my head.

"I know about family blood too. Dexter is like family and no one messes with family."

A man emerged from the side of the Camaro. The blinding lights of the headlights didn't allow me to make out the figure. He was aiming a rifle in our direction.

"No one messes with my family."

It was The Don.

# Chapter 51

The Don walked up to the hooded man and blew a baseball sized hole through his chest. It was like he'd planned this for years with no hesitation. John shielded his eyes from blood splatter and covered ears from the noise of the automatic weapon.

"I didn't like this one. He was a pain in my ass. Didn't have the chops to be a true Buffone," said the Don, standing over the body puffing his chest out with much pride.

He limped over and picked up my plastic tied arms. The Don was strong for being short, fat, and old. I felt my shoulder blades bend beyond their natural position. He stared down John, "Don't even think about it, fatty. I'm taking your sidekick with me," he said, dragging me along the gravel and pavement.

John's ears still ringing from the gun blast nodded in agreement and didn't make a move. He crept back toward the crumpled truck holding his banged up shoulder that was dislocated in the crash.

The Don yanked me up like a helpless ball of human and flung me into the backseat of the Camaro. I laid on my back and winced with the pressure of my shoulders getting tighter. Stared at the grey ceiling upholstery and my eyes became blurry with spots and blood.

I thought about John standing on the side of the highway with the truck smashed to pieces. Not sure what to do. He wasn't the quickest thinker on his feet. One time we pulled into a drive through for a burger and we ended leaving because he froze deciding between fries or onion rings.

My mind flashed to the morning when I picked up my father in prison. Filled with so much hope about the possibility of having him in my life for a season.

Gone.

I thought about Samantha hurt by my lies sitting in a hotel room alone, sad, and scared. My family the only rock in this crazy life, fractured, and bleeding like my banged up face.

"Good to see you again, paison," the Don said, nursing his right collarbone.

I didn't talk.

"You thought you had us at the church, right?"

I shifted on the seat trying to get comfortable as the ties dug into my skin.

"There's a lot of bodies piled up at the church.

I'm not sure what your version of success looks like?" I said, knowing I wanted the Don dead. Head of the snake.

Bloody tissues were piling up on the middle console of the car. He rubbed his shoulder and placed one over his buttoned white shirt.

"That's a lot of blood."

"You got a lucky shot off while your fat friend was nuking everyone with his garage door opener."

"It's not a garage door opener. It's an electromagnetic... never mind."

"You might think you were successful back at the church. But I don't care about those men. They were just pawns in a larger chess game."

"What do you mean? I'd be pretty upset if a bunch of my family we're murdered in cold blood. I know what that feels like."

The Don chuckled and placed a couple more tissues on his wounded shoulder, "Family? You think those incompetent chumps were family? Nope. LeClaire PD. They owed me a favor."

I thought of the six men we killed knowing they were LPD and I got sick to my stomach. These men knew my family and vice versa.

"If these men are not family. Where's yours hiding?"

"Oh... wouldn't you like to know? Why, so you and the fat guy can sneak up on them? They are safe and sound. We Buffone's try not to impede unnecessary violence," he said, chewing on a toothpick and giving a smile.

"That's the biggest pile of shit I've heard in a while. You and your family have been hurting and ripping people off in LeClaire for decades. I don't know what Buffone means, but violence is probably in its etymology."

"Buffone's are a peaceful people. It's only when one of them gets murdered that we have problems. Your dad might know something about that."

"The only peace for your family will be when you're dead and gone."

"Big words, for a small man. How are you doing after we killed your father? Peaceful?"

I bit my lip and tried to not say what was in my head, "The O'Kane's are a peaceful people too. We don't act kindly toward cowards who kill old men for thirty-year-old debts. Maybe we have more in common than I thought..."

I felt one of my hands shake loose from the plastic tie. Clenched it and bent it awkwardly to slip it through the loop. Kept the loose hand hidden behind my back.

"Dexter... Dexter... We bent over backwards for your father. He had every opportunity to pay off those debts. Unfortunately... time ran out."

"There's still time... for you and your family to not get killed. I'd think about your next move."

"Funny. I think you're the one tied up and not

in a position to make these kinds of threats. Think about your next move."

I felt the car slow down and pull to a stop. The Don opened the back door and yanked me from the car. I pretended both hands locked in the ties.

"We made it," the Don said, guiding me toward the front of a building.

"Can you check my ties and make sure they're attached?"

The Don glanced down at my wrists and became wide eyed when my fist was untethered.

I stood to my feet and gave him a left hook to the stomach. My fist swallowed up by layers of fat from years of eating meat ball sandwiches and manicotti.

He bent over after the wind being knocked out of his pudgy belly. He slumped to his knees on the gravel ground. Rifle falling to the side.

I wiped dirt and blood from my face and looked up at the large sign on the building.

Antique Adventures.

# Chapter 52

I peered through the doors of Antique Adventures broken glass crunched beneath my feet. The inside of the store looked like a tornado had landed and vomited rusty gold to every corner of the space.

I made my way through the mess to the back of the store. I pushed a back door of the store and peeked into the storage area. This is where we clean, varnish, and repair antiques before selling them in the store, or online. I heard small whimpers like a puppy caught in the cold come from a corner of the dark storage area.

"Hello? Who's here? I'm armed and want no trouble," I said, with my pretend gun.

My dog bolted across the dark room and crashed into my legs. He whimpered and looked up with sad eyes.

Beams of light from the moon cast shadows across metal beams in the rafters. I locked eyes on an object high in the ceiling.

A body swayed side-to-side light bouncing off the corpse. The noose wrapped around the neck, cuts on her face, and no signs of life.

It was Elizabeth.

A handwritten note hung across the dead body pinned against her red dress.

"We need our money, Dexter. The interest is running. Next time it'll be your wife."

I heard tightening of rope as the body swung above my head. Found a knife, climbed a ladder, and cut down Elizabeth.

A tear welled up in my eye.

I was tired.

Sparky barked behind me.

# Chapter 53

I felt the cold steel of a rifle press into the back of my head. My dog barked and growled at the man coming out of the shadows. He smelled of mint gum and cheap cologne. The Don.

I raised my hands dropping the knife on the cement floor making a loud crash. The dog kept barking, "Shut up mutt," the Don said, turning to yell at me, "Shut him up, or he gets a bullet between the ears."

"Buster...it's okay buddy. Be nice to the bad man," I said, leaning down to pet Buster, and then looked up to smile at the Don.

The dog kept yapping and went for his leg. The Don shook him off and aimed the gun between his ears.

BOOM.

The dog yelped and fell over.

"You son of a bitch," I said, holding my hands in the sky staring at Buster's and Elizabeth's bodies on the floor.

"I'm not a dog guy, more of a cat guy. Especially ones that bite," the Don said, with a grin.

"So what's your next move Italian piece of shit? You killed my dog and Elizabeth. Now you think I will pay my father's debts. I don't think so."

"If you only knew how much power I have in LeClaire. It is kind of mind blowing. You can pay now... or it might happen in the night, back alley, or when you're playing with your kids. Those debts paid. Or I take it out of your wife's ass. Samantha is it?"

"Shoot me right now if you think it'll happen."

"How do you know it hasn't?"

"I have pull in this city too. Let's not pretend you're the only one running things in LeClaire. I know people."

I heard the snapping of gum in my ear. The Don's hot breath blew on my neck sending chills down my spine. "Dexter, Dexter. Don't think I won't kill your wife like I did your father, Peter, and Elizabeth. And, I'll get away with it too. The police owe me a lot of favors... if you know what I mean..." he said, looking down at Elizabeth on the floor.

"Don't talk about them anymore. You're gonna regret it."

The Don pushed the gun into my skull and I could feel the bones in my head shifting, "Is that a threat?"

"A promise."

"I'll put my track record against yours any day. LeClaire's under my thumb," he said, examining his thumb.

The keys in my pocket shifted while one stabbed the leg. It gave me an idea.

"Let's say... I know people in LeClaire who handle these kinds of situations."

"Who would that be?"

"Me."

I swung my left hand down on the keys in my pocket. The pressure set off the panic button on my alarm for the store. The room lit up with lights and sound. I turned and punched the Don in the teeth; blood spewing onto an old lamp sitting on a wooden chair.

He staggered back and dropped the gun on the floor. The alarm blared in our ears and he tried to cover them while gaining his balance.

I dove toward the gun on the floor, gripped the gun, and fired two shots in The Don's direction.

The Don's eyes widened at the shock of the bullets piercing his flabby stomach. Blood grew in concentric circles through his shirt. He fell to his knees, the gum falling out of his mouth, into a pool of blood.

The Don's head laid next to my dog.

"You don't mess with man's best friend."

I pressed the clicker on the alarm and the store went silent. I slouched in a chair and tried to catch my breath.

# Chapter 54

The rain beaded up on my black North Face jacket. It was a joint funeral for the Chief and Elizabeth. I sat in the wooden chair thinking about Peter, Dad, Lisa, and Spencer. Funerals brought me back to days I'd rather have forgotten. If they were giving out attendance stars for funerals, I'd be the champ of late.

The pastor spoke of hope and heaven. A mix of quiet sobs and yelping came from cousins, siblings, aunts, uncles, and the people of LeClaire. No matter who you are the funeral brings out contemplation on what matters in life and the reality we are finite.

But I was not in a contemplative mood. I'd be lying if the anger in my chest was not ready to explode and lead to a multitude of sins. I shook my head, stared at the soaked grass, and examined the hundreds of people in attendance. The pastor recited a portion of the Lord's Prayer:

"Forgive us our sins... and those who have sinned against us."

A picture of my father appeared in my mind followed by the Don. I couldn't make the connections of the murders in the last few days. Too many people involved and couldn't draw a straight line for what to do next. There was no way the Don's involved alone. He had a lot of help.

The bodies laid in the ground as a police officer for LeClaire PD played a trumpet. People dispersed into the afternoon and I wandered on the lawn trying to recharge after putting on an extroverted front while living an introverted life.

A young man, about twenty-three, short spiked hair wandered over while I picked a hanging leaf on a tree, "You Dexter O'Kane?"

I noticed a tattoo on the inside of his forearm that read Buffone in cursive, "That's what my mother called me before she died. Sorry... too much?"

The young man surprised by my response he stared at the ground, "I might know things that could be helpful to you."

"Please don't fuck with me right now. The last time I attended a funeral I beat the shit out of a guy. I hope you're not looking for a fight. If not, can you at least tell me why anyone who gets near me dies?"

He jammed hands in his slack pockets ignoring my honest rambling, "I know who's behind the killings."

I smiled and pretended that his comments were not naïve, "I do too. The Buffone family," I said, pointing at his tattooed arm.

"Not exactly."

Intrigued, I asked for him to tell me more. The young man held out his hand, "I'm not a psycho. Name's Luke Buffone."

"So the tattoo is not an ex-girlfriend? You're part of the Buffone family? Tell me why I shouldn't kill you right here. Place your body in a hole right over there," I said, pointing to a fresh grave plot about thirty yards away.

"I know my family are bad people. They've been causing trouble in LeClaire for the last thirty years. But I'm just a distant cousin. My mother married into the Family, but she divorced years ago, and we tried to steer clear. The problems complicated."

"You care to share?"

The young man continued to look everywhere but in my eyes, "You swear not to tell? My mother doesn't even know I'm talking to you. If anyone finds out I'm dead and everyone else in my life."

I crossed my fingers giving the official I swear sign, "Elizabeth hired you to kill the Don and his crew. She knew they were messing with the Chief and he owed them favors. But the Buffone's were not behind these murders. A police officer in the LPD was. There are so many people in the family the Don doesn't even know who's doing what.

He probably didn't understand who was committing the murders."

"Who?" I asked, with piqued interest.

"His name is Larry Nelson. He's been on the force for over ten years. Born and raised in LeClaire. The family often took officers under their wing and paid them good money to pull jobs on the side. Larry never got selected for the jobs and became bitter. He took matters into his own hands and framed the Buffone's."

I grabbed my chin and thought about all the officers I had encountered in the last couple of weeks, "Did he have a flat top?"

"Yep. How did you know?"

"I've run into him quite a few times in the last couple of months."

"Be careful. This guy is twisted and looking for revenge."

"Know where I can find him?"

We exchanged numbers, and he texted me an address. "This is his home. Please don't mention this conversation to anyone. He's a sick dude. I want no part of this stuff. But I felt I needed to help you and the people of LeClaire."

I thanked the young man.

I knew my next move.

# Chapter 55

A late snow called on LeClaire. Not common for March. Streets were icy with a fresh layer of snow dust piling up on the concrete and dirt. John and I sat in the F-150 not saying much.

Hoped this would all end tonight. Needed a nap.

I bumped John's fist and we loaded out the truck. The house was dark, and no cars were in the driveway. We scanned the street left and right.

Quiet.

I waved John over; he went to the left of the house, and I went up the driveway on the right. I wondered if this was the right house because of the darkness. Maybe the young man was pulling my leg and gave a bad lead? Not what we needed tonight.

I sat under a window on the right side of the house. The drops of new snow dripped off the tip of my nose and gun. I stood up and peeked into what appeared to be a bedroom. The lights were not on and the house looked empty.

I waved John over to the front of the house. We

stood on the porch at a white front door. The mail-box was full of mail and newspapers piled on the ground.

I counted 1-2-3 and kicked in the door.

"Larry? Larry Nelson? You home? This is your friends Dexter and John. You might remember me from visits to my place in the last few weeks. Please come out if you are here... We need to talk."

Silence.

"Larry, come out, we need to chat for a minute," I said.

John shook his head knowing no one was home. I punched on a light and looked around.

The living room covered with photos hanging on every wall. Inked arrows connecting the pic-tures from one to the other. A coffee table piled high with newspapers and articles like a journalist investigating an important story.

I picked up one article and noticed it circled in red ink. The headline story in the LeClaire Gazette was about the death of Peter.

I showed John.

"This place looks like that scene in Beautiful Minds. I think we're dealing with a psycho," John said, examining the photos on the wall.

I walked around the sterile room only graced with pictures and papers and no furniture. There were small scribbles and notes on each one.

I leaned in to the wall and tried to see the pic-tures up close, "Oh shit," I said.

John came over and looked at the photo I was examining, "That's you and your family, Dexter."

The picture looked like it was taken with a camera from across the street of our house. He was watching us and had plans to kill us. At least that's what I think.

I walked up and down the hall and each photo crossed out with a marker. Each mark was another death. My father, Peter, Chief, and the Don, all crossed out. The picture of my family still unmarked.

"He's going after my family," I said, a sense of panic set in, and I ran out of the house to call my wife.

# Chapter 56

"**D**ammit, come on."

I slapped my cell phone and wanted to throw it out a window when a call wouldn't go through. I motioned for John to give me his phone.

The phone rang. Voicemail.

"Samantha...this is Dexter. You need to get the boys and your mom out of the motel. There's a terrible man who might look for you. Meet me at the lake house in thirty minutes. The key is under the pot on the porch. Please call, or text John's, or my phone when you get this..."

I hung up the phone and texted the same message for good measure.

The lake house a small gift to my family after business at Antique Adventures boomed the last couple of years. It was only forty minutes outside of LeClaire at one of the better lakes in Missouri, Lake Grand.

"She didn't answer. I'm freaking out," I said, fiddling with the keys trying to start the truck.

John slapped me on the shoulder and tried to comfort me, "Samantha is a tough chick. She will be fine. I'm sure the family is fine and will call back any minute. We'll find 'em."

My phone buzzed between my legs. I ripped it out of the nether regions and almost dropped it on the floor. "Samantha... Samantha... You okay?"

I could tell she was groggy coming out of sleep or was just tired, "We're fine. What's going on?"

"Did you get my text?"

"I didn't look. What's up?"

"There's a terrible man looking for you. You need to get out of the motel and get to the lake house. You'll be safe there, for now."

"Who's trying to hurt us?"

"It doesn't matter. But, if any suspicious people with flattops come by... run," I said, as the phone cut out losing battery power. I hit it with my hand. "Samantha... Samantha... dammit!"

A tear ran down the side of my stubbled cheek. "Everything okay?" John asked, with wide eyes of concern.

"I don't know... told them to leave the motel for the lake house. Hope Samantha moves in a hurry."

I pressed on the gas focusing on the highway and tried to not think about the worst.

# Chapter 57

A knock rattled the hotel door. Samantha peeked around the corner of the door to see an officer standing in the hallway.

"Sorry to bother you ma'am. I'm patrolling the hotel after a domestic violence call. Have you seen a tall man wandering the halls by chance?"

"No, sir. We've been in the room all day."

"Ma'am... do you mind if I ask you a few questions?"

The officer placed his hand at the top of the door and applied pressure. "Like I said, we've been inside all day. We need to get trouble,rest, thank you," Samantha said, trying to close the door.

The officer shoved his foot into the door and pushed it open with force. Samantha fell back the corner of the door catching her forehead. She sized up the man as she slammed into the wall.

"I'm sorry having to get rough. But, I need to ask you a question..." said, the officer.

Samantha's mother placed her arms over the

pack and play and backed into the corner of the small room, "Please leave us alone. We know nothing," she said.

The officer pulled out his pistol and aimed at Samantha, her mother, and waved it back toward the hallway, "We're all going on a little trip. I need to ask questions down at the station. If you give me any more trouble, I will use a different force," he said.

Kids awoke and cried, "Can I at least feed my boys before we leave? Please...they are hungry...we are not a threat."

The officer looked at Samantha, walked to the twins and peeked into their cribs watching them cry. He looked back at Samantha, "Feed them in the car. We are leaving now."

Samantha fed the twins in the back of a police cruiser while the sirens blared. The officer ran a comb through his flat top.

# Chapter 58

I stopped at the Barn to load up the truck with ammunition, weapons, and extra protection. I had an in-between peace that Samantha was okay and still wanted to hurry to ensure she was.

John rummaged through a box of electrical components examining wires sticking out of a small device. He held up another garage-door-opener-looking-thing with a sense of pride.

"New and improved. Works like a charm. I needed to tweak the power switch with an American-made component. Tried to save a few bucks with foreign parts and it broke," John said, tossing the device in my direction.

Turned the device over in my hand and pretended I knew what I was looking at, "Nice. Looks good."

"Check out the top."

I flipped the device over examining two wires coming out of the small white device, "What do those do?"

"The deluxe model has backup power. If the electrodes don't kill the enemy first try. You have a second option. A taser. These wires burst out of the top and inject into the bad guy," John said, pointing at the device.

I nodded my head pretending I cared. I held up my pistol, "This works good too..."

"Mine is more humane."

"Mine is more fun," I said, as we both laughed.

I kneeled on the floor and called John to join me. "What are you doing?"

"I'm not sure. Just know I'm not in a good place and need Divine help."

I set the pistol on the cold cement floor, looked up to heaven, and prayed the Lord's Prayer. Realized I heard this prayer from many pastors and priests in the last few weeks at all the funerals.

A peace came over me for the first time in a long time... at least for a moment.

"Amen."

# Chapter 59

T he road to Lake Grand curved to the right and then to the left. The headlights of the truck lit up trees, small cabins, and small eyes scuffling in the forest. There was a small layer of snow on the road making the truck slip. in each turn.

We pulled up to a black iron gate. I leaned out of the truck window and punched in the numbers to the security gate. The gate yawned open, and I tapped my jeans in nervous waiting.

John laid his gun across his lap and placed the white garage door opener in an inside jacket pocket. I fiddled with my gun holstered on my hip.

The lights of the truck flashed up onto the porch of the lake house as we approached. House dark and quiet.

I scanned the property looking for signs of life, "I don't think they're here yet."

I parked the truck in a driveway off the side of the house. We walked up the wide wooden steps of the house and I wrestled my keys out of my pocket. My heart pounded.

The lights of the house burst on like someone just turned on stadium lights for the Kansas City Chiefs.

John and I shielded our eyes and tried to see through the blindness into the living room. I saw two figures gagged and tied to chairs in the middle of the room.

My eyes filled with spots trying to adjust to the light. The porch floor covered with floodlights and extension cords sprawled in every direction.

A man stood in between the two figures, "Hello Dexter and John. I thought you might show up here. You seem like family guys. Nice place here..." the man said, scanning the logged cabin.

I shielded my eyes and reached for my pistol not sure who I was looking at. We moved in closer where the light was not as intense.

A man wearing an LPD uniform aimed a pistol at me and John. He held another object in his left hand, "Do you want to die with a bullet or from this little guy?" he said, waving a garage door opener.

"Where did you get that?" John asked.

"I visited your barn and found some interesting plans for this little gizmo. I've never used it on a human... yet. But I think I got the hang of it. Who wants to be first?"

My heart beat into my throat. I looked at Samantha and tears were spilling out of her soft blue eyes. Her mother slumped over in the chair.

"What do you want from us? The Buffone family are the ones you should want to kill. Why my dad? Why Peter?"

"Dexter... Dexter... I hate those greasy Italians. They took everything from me. They're a bunch of lying thieves. A ticket out of this shitty town. It didn't work out as planned."

"Leave my family out of this. If you want to deal with me... fine... but let them go," I said.

"Lower the gun, Dexter. You don't want to shrink your family today," the officer said, holding the small device to the temple of Samantha.

"From what I understand these wires will fry her in a second, correct?"

I didn't respond.

I slipped my finger on the trigger and pushed in a little more, "You still didn't answer my question. Why us? We hurt no one."

"When did you graduate high school?"

"Ugh... 94'."

"South LeClaire High?"

"Yeah."

"I graduated in 1995."

I thought for a second and didn't recognize the flat-topped officer. We all gain a few pounds over the years.

"What's your name?"

"Nelson."

It became clear in a flash, "Oh, shit. You're Bubba Nelson?"

Bubba Nelson (real name Larry) was the most overweight junior at my high school. Tortured in school more ways than one. I dated his sister.

"That's me."

I shook my head and smiled, "You lost a lot of weight. I didn't even recognize you," I said, giving a look up and down at his chiseled body.

"Thanks. I've been training for twenty years. Waiting for the right moment. The moment is now."

I scratched my head and didn't understand what was going on, "Did I call you fat in high school, or something? I'm not sure why you're so pissed and want me dead. If I did... sorry," I said, with an insincere apology.

"You remember prom 1994?"

I thought for a second and tried to recall twenty years of memories, "I remember taking..."

"Taking my sister to the prom? And ditching her that night for Lisa?"

Lisa was my first wife.

# Chapter 60

The creaking of old wood floors echoed through the lake house. The women whimpered, and we were getting tired.

"Listen... you don't need to kill me and my family over something that happened in high school. Isn't that kind of overkill? Let's should'veput it behind us and move on..."

"My family was everything. I know you get that. You wounded my sister and our family because of your selfishness."

"How's your sister doing?"

The officer paused a beat, "She's dead."

"Oh..."

"Committed suicide because of you. She loved you and you dropped her like a bad habit. When Mary heard you married Lisa, she put a bullet in her head."

My stomach ached thinking about Nelson's sister, "Wow... I had no idea. Why didn't I hear about it? News in LeClaire spreads fast."

"Our family moved to Washington after graduation. My dad transferred for work."

I sighed.

"So here we are, Dexter. The moment I've waited for. Lisa is dead, and looks like you will be a single dad again, at least for a moment. Even better. How can it being any sweeter? I hope this forces you to rethink the value of people and life."

"Where are my boys, daughter?"

"Don't worry, I thought ahead. I knew they would grow up without a daddy and mommy. I dropped them at Social Services. You can thank me later."

I squeezed the trigger a little more and my body got warm with rage. John still held his pistol steady at the officer's head.

"Let's not get ahead of ourselves. After I kill you, we can pick them up on the way home," I said.

"Here we go again. The true Dexter. You selfish piece of shit, always arrogant, always cocky. Thinking you can get out of any situation. Treat people like trash and get away with it. Not anymore..."

"Bubba... I'm not that guy anymore. People change. It was high school, we were all selfish. I didn't mean to hurt your sister. And, I'm sorry for your loss. You don't need to do this..."

"You should've thought of that before you dumped my sister. I don't need your little speeches. Time is out."

I jammed my boot in the ground, bit my lip, and

tried not to fire a bullet right through his smirking face too soon. He held the device against Samantha's head.

"Don't do it," I said.

I squinted my left eye over the pistol and aimed right between Larry's eyes. His hand trembled squeezing the device veins bulging.

"Sorry it had to end like this. But I think losing your wife will be more devastating. You can think about what you did to my sister for the rest of your sad life," Larry said, pressing the garage door opener.

Nothing.

He hit the side of the device and mumbled under his breath, "Are you shitting me? This piece of crap doesn't work."

John yelled out, "It's a prototype. I'm still working out the bugs."

Larry raised his pistol in the other hand and shot John, knocking him to the ground. He turned and fired on me hitting me in the shoulder.

I fired a bullet in his direction. I don't know if it hit.

He ran to the back of the house out of sight.

Heard a door slam.

I stood over John not moving.

Assessed the wound in my shoulder. Blood poured out.

# Chapter 61

I checked on Samantha and her mother slumped in chairs and shaken. Untied them and locked them in a back bedroom. "Don't leave this room. I'll come back and get you," I said, pulling a bookcase across the door.

I headed toward where Larry ran off. Stood against the door of a bathroom and I leaned in with my ear, "Larry? You in there? There's no way out of here. I will either break down the door and kill you, or you'll bleed out from your wound," I said, staring at a trail of blood leading into the bathroom.

The bathroom was quiet with only the hum of a light fixture. "If you're still alive Larry, please say something so I don't have to shoot you again. You're going to jail for a long time or rotting in hell, or both," I said with a grin.

Silence.

I stepped back from the bathroom door and fired three shots; high, middle, low, for added measure. Shards of wood exploded inside the room and an echo trailed. I pushed on the door, glanced inside, and noticed a pool of blood on a white mat in the center of the tiled floor.

A window above the toilet propped open at the far end of the bathroom. Trail of blood crawled up the side of the wall. The cool breeze from the lake pushed in from the window. I stood up on the toilet and peeked out into the forest-lined lake to look for Larry.

The dust and taillights of what appeared to be a police cruiser vanished into the distance.

I ran back into the living room and John was still unconscious on the floor. I called for an ambulance and told Samantha and her mother to stay put for the paramedics and police to arrive.

"Dexter...be careful," Samantha said, giving me a tight embrace that seemed to last for an hour.

"I will. No one messes with the O'Kane's and gets away with it," I said, checking a clip in my pistol.

# Chapter 62

The truck marched down the highway not sure where I was headed. Daydreamed about my father when I picked him up in prison. Hope for a normal family one day. Dreamed about a grandpa holding my twins in his arms and taking them to the park, and Royals games.

I drove miles not aware... I was driving. The trees, cars, and people passed through my eyes like they didn't exist. I was numb. Wanted to kill Larry more than anything. Needed everything done. Wanted a nap. And wanted the Buffone's to leave LeClaire and harass s different community.

I turned on a police scanner LeClaire PD gave me as a gift for help with a job. Played with the nobs trying to find a clear signal.

"Local dispatch. This is forty-nine calling on a breaking and entering possible homicide. We need paramedics and police at 413 Pine Ave."

A familiar voice came over the airwaves, "This is

Larry Nelson, LeClaire PD. I'm in the area. I'll head to the scene."

"Thank you, please be safe."

"I'll need backup if any other officers are in the area."

LeClaire is not a hotbed of criminal activity. Unless you include cow tipping and stealing tractors. The public service agencies can often be familial and informal.

I slammed my hand against the steering wheel. I knew Larry was trying to set me up, "That asshole. He's going back to the lake house."

Yanked the steering wheel and flipped a U-Turn and headed back to the lake house. Laid open the clip in my gun to make sure enough bullets. I heard another call on the police scanner.

"This is Charlie Rodriguez, LeClaire PD. I'd like to report an assault."

"This is dispatch. How can we help?"

"My partner in the LPD, Larry Nelson, attacked me, stole my cruiser, and left me on the side of the road. I don't know where he's going or what is wrong with him. He's acting strange."

"I'll call LPD for look out of the car and the officer. Did you say Larry Nelson?"

"Yes."

"That's odd. He called in to help with a situation at Lake Grand."

"Lake Grand?"

"Yes. That's where the address called in from."

"I'm at Lake Grand. Stranded for hours at Dickey's Roadside Diner."

"We'll send someone to pick you up, shortly."

"Thank you. Please come quick as my partner has lost his marbles."

I sped down the highway and knew exactly where the officer was. We'd spent many family breakfasts at this greasy spoon on trips to the lake. Best pancakes in LeClaire County.

I saw the officer sitting at the front of the diner with an ice pack on his swollen face.

I leaned out of the window of the truck, "Hey, get in."

"Who are you?" he said, trying to adjust his eyes as I leaned over the edge of the truck door.

"Dexter O'Kane. It's not important right now. Get in. I know where Larry is..."

"Oh, shit. I know you. You're the guy who got a brick through the window a couple weeks ago."

"That's me."

"How do you know Larry?"

"I dated his sister. Just get in and I'll explain on the way."

I examined the wounds on the face of the officer. It looked like he went twelve rounds and got knocked out by Mike Tyson.

"You and your partner have a domestic dispute?"

"Larry's lost his mind. He told me about some property he would buy at Lake Grand and wanted me to check it out. We stopped in at the diner and he punched my lights out. I think he needs a vacation. He's been acting off for a few months."

"I think he's more than crazy..."

"How do you know him other than dating his sister?"

"Never met the guy until you guys kept showing up at my house. I dated his sister over twenty years ago. Long story."

"You got a weapon on you?"

"I'm LPD," the officer said, waving his gun.

"You'll need it. Larry is not in a happy place. This could get ugly."

The officer pulled the washcloth and ice away from his face and looked at me with raised eyebrows, "You know I'm an officer of the law, correct? I don't need a civilian taking things into their own hands. I know we live in a small town, but the law is the law."

"We will break a few laws tonight if we want to stop your crazy partner. Trust me on this one. Let me explain..."

# Chapter 63

After explaining my history with Officer Larry his partner didn't care about laws any longer. He wanted him stopped as much as I did.

We pulled back into the lake house and waited for Larry and back-up to arrive. John was sitting up in the living room and Samantha was tending to his wound. He was groggy and asked about what happened. We moved him onto a bed in the back bedroom with Sam and her mother.

I waited with the officer in the front room for Larry. We heard the crushing of gravel under tires as the police cruiser pulled into the driveway.

We pulled our weapons.

Larry stumbled up the steps with a stamp of red growing on his right shoulder through his LPD uniform.

The partner and I aimed our pistols at Larry waiting for him to open the door, "This is Officer Nelson, LPD. I'm responding to a possible break in... hello? Is anyone in here?"

Larry creaked open the door and did not see us crouched in the corner of the great room.

I could sense the irrational nature of Larry's posture as he continued to ask questions. Like he didn't know where he was.

"This is Officer Nelson from LeClaire, PD. Anyone here? I'm responding to a break in."

His partner looked at me puzzled and gripped his pistol tighter. "What is wrong with this guy?" he mouthed at me.

"If anyone is here. Please come out with your hands up and you'll won't be hurt. I don't want to use force," Larry said, in a formal police manner.

"Hey Nelson... Rodriguez here. I know what you did. I know what you did to those families. Let's not do anything stupid now to make things worse."

"Good to hear your voice... coward. How's your face? Hope we can still be friends after this."

"Coward? I'm not sure who the coward is. You punched me while I was eating a pancake. Friends... I don't think so, bro."

"It's fine. I have plenty of friends. Besides, I always hated you... you stupid Mexican. The worst partner I've had in the last ten years. Your incompetence is astounding."

"Good to hear your racism is still intact."

"You're damn right. People like you come to America, from their grass huts and dusty villages, take our jobs, women, and make us pay more taxes. Who needs you?"

Rodriguez whispered in my ear, "If I have to hear about this one more time. I'll put a bullet in my might'vehead," he said, trying to hold back laughter.

We crouched in the corner of the room with guns drawn in the shadows. The only light coming through the front windows from the moon. Larry didn't know we were only a few feet away.

I lined my pistol between his brown eyes and placed a finger on the trigger. My hand trembled as my heart beat fast.

"Larry. Dexter here. There's no way out of the mess you've gotten yourself in. I've called the authorities and the house will swarm with cops any minute."

The lake house lit up with reds, whites, and loud beeps. Ambulances and police cruisers surrounded the front of the house, "I wasn't lying."

"Go to hell... Dexter. You and your family. Let's not pretend you are innocent. You took away my sister. I don't know how you sleep at night."

"I'll sleep fine. The blood is on your hands and not mine."

Larry wobbled his gun side to side and grimaced with pain from the gunshot wound in his shoulder, "Before this shit ends. Someone else needs to die. That someone is you... O'Kane."

He fired a bullet into the air not knowing where we stood. He wobbled like a drunk closing down

O'Malley's and he fired again taking down a deer chandelier crashing to the floor.

Before I could get a shot off Larry fell to the ground in a heap.

Police officers rushed into the house thinking they were investigating a break in, "We had a call from this address. Is everything okay?" a short officer said, glancing down at Larry laying on the floor.

"We're okay. This man broke in and tried to hurt my family," I said, tapping Larry with my boot. "I'm thinking heart attack. He fell over."

Two EMT's with a gurney rushed into the lake house. One leaned over the body and listened for breath sounds. He looked up at his partner and shook his head, "I'm not getting anything," he said, starting chest compressions.

A detective asked the typical questions of my family.

My wife and mother taken to the hospital to make sure they were okay from a few minor injuries.

I walked to the back bedroom as they were working on John. He looked up at me and smiled, "Did you get him?" John asked, in between a cough.

"Weird thing. I think he died of a heart attack. We were in a gun fight and he Rodriguezkeeled over," I said.

"You okay big fella?"

"A little sore... but I'll live."

I glanced down into John's hand. The garage

door opener was in between his fingers. I grabbed my chin and pretended to be thinking deep, "I think I know what happened," I said, ripping the opener from John.

"It might've been a heart attack for another reason," John said, with a grin.

"I thought it was only a prototype?" I asked.

"Well...looks like I might've worked the kinks out. We might be on to something."

I looked up at the EMT, "Take good care of this guy. He's family."

"We will do our best," a brown haired woman said.

I placed the garage door opener in my pocket and gave a laugh and then a sigh.

I need that nap.

# Chapter 64

L ater that evening we sat in a hospital room and watched John sleep. The doctors were confident of a full recovery. I smiled thinking about his stupid garage door opener that saved our lives hours earlier. Samantha sat next to me in an overstuffed chair and rubbed my hand.

"Dex... can we go on a vacation?"

"Where you want to go? I hear Kansas City has cool stuff to see."

"No. That's not what I meant. Ugh, like, a vacation from this," Samantha said, pointing to John, and me.

"I don't follow."

A small tear formed in the corner of Samantha's eye and her hands became clammy, "Can we take a vacation from chasing bad guys? This one scared me... a lot."

I gripped her hand feeling them tremble. My heart raced as I saw the fear in her eyes, "I told you... I would never put you in a situation where'd you live in fear. Things got out of hand. I thought reconnecting with my dad was the right thing to do. It was NOT," I said, with a chuckle.

"It's not just about your father. This is not the life I signed up for. I want you to run Antique Adventures, be a good husband, and father. Nothing more, nothing less."

I turned to John, and back to Samantha, not sure what to say. The pull of the side-gig was stronger than I ever expected. I didn't want to hurt Samantha, and I still wanted to stop bad guys.

"Why don't we take a real vacation? Get our heads right and let the dust settle. I know I could use one after this drama."

Her eyes told me this was not satisfactory, and she stared at the floor, "I wish you'd think about me more, and less protecting LeClaire. I feel like everything else gets precedence, and the family gets leftovers."

She was right. I was a cowboy. Didn't want to be tied down and was always looking for the next cow to rope and hill to climb. Met Samantha after the death of my wife and needed stability. I didn't know how to walk the tight rope of crime fighter, business, and family, "I... know... I can be selfish. Trying to reconnect with my dad was not selfish. Was it?"

"No. But I need you to be around more than you are. You will lose us."

Samantha placed a pacifier in one of the twin's

mouth and looked back at me with tears ruining her makeup. "There's something I need to tell you."

"Go ahead."

Samantha left her chair and stepped into the hallway. She came back with a young man about thirteen. He wore a white hoodie, baggy jeans, and didn't smile.

"Who's this young buck?" I asked.

Samantha kissed the boy on the side of the head, "He's my son."

My knees buckled for a second and the words didn't compute the first time through my ears, "Your son? Is this a joke?"

She hugged the boy and his emotions on his face were missing amidst his acne scarred cheeks, "When I was fifteen I got pregnant. Ronnie taken away from me because I was not a fit mother according to Social Services. He's raised by a distant uncle in southern Missouri."

"What does this mean?" I asked, turning down the volume of the TV.

Samantha paused a second and I could see her planning words, "I want to see if Ronnie can live with us. He's been in foster care after my uncle died. I want to see if we can make it work. I'm asking you to take a vacation and focus on the family."

For whatever reason the offer didn't seem crazy. I loved Samantha and would do anything to keep her in my life. Knew my selfishness was a problem but knew we could get through anything life threw at us.

I raised my hand to the shy teenager, "Hi Ronnie. My name is Dexter and I'm your mother's husband. Nice to meet you."

He handed me a dead fish handshake and gave a quiet hello, "I know this must be hard. But Samantha is the best mother I know and takes great care of her boys," I said, looking down at the twins sleeping in their car seats.

He nodded and jammed his hands further into his hoodie pockets.

Samantha said, "Ronnie will stay with us for the weekend and the agency will give us a few weeks to determine family fit. What do you think? Can we try?"

John opened his eyes and turned his head toward me, "Hey Dex... where am I? Who is that?"

I looked at Samantha and then back at John with a smile, "Samantha's son."

"How long have I been asleep? Aren't your twins like eighteen months or something?"

We laughed, "Yes. This is Ronnie. We're hanging out this weekend. If that's cool with him?"

He nodded yes.

Adding one more family member to the O'Kane clan didn't matter. I loved these crazy people. You don't choose your family and you gotta deal with it.

But deep inside I was selfish. I knew it. I wasn't ready to leave my second life.

# Chapter 65

The waiter came to the table speaking in a thick Italian accent. I peeked down at a menu and weighed the options of spaghetti or lasagna, "Lasagna. I heard it's the best in LeClaire."

"Oh yes, sir. The Buffone family uses our grandmother's recipe to make the best Italian food in the city," she said, scribbling on a note pad.

I smirked and looked around the table with a sense of peace and joy not felt in a long time. Ronnie pulled apart a massive piece of garlic bread and dipped it in a plate of oils. The twins giggled and made their typical little boy sounds while my daughter made faces at them. Samantha sat back in the red booth and laughed when John told another inappropriate single guy joke.

I sipped on my water and chewed on a piece of ice watching the table. Everything felt right in the world.

At least in LeClaire... for the night... or was it?

# How to make an author crazy grateful?

If you liked this book, and want to see more in the series, I can help. And, there are some things you can do that will help me out a ton:

(1) **Review this Book**

Go to wherever you purchased this title, and leave an honest review. You have no idea how that helps me keep writing and publishing. I want to build a rabid tribe of fans that want more of my stuff. Reviews are essential!

(2) **Become a VIP**

VIP's are what I call the people on my mailing list. They get latest updates on book releases, blog posts, and (best of all... wait for it) FREE GIVE-AWAYS!

Become a VIP today.

(3) **Get the Next Book in the Series**

The adventures of Dexter and John continue in *Color Blind (Book 3)*. Dexter and John are on another wild adventure when a racist cult comes to town. They must stop the spread of their wicked message and not to mention murders, before they brainwash and destroy LeClaire. Laughs loud, and body count high!

Thanks for your help, and thanks for reading!

Cheers,

Ryan J. Pelton

# Author's Note

Families are dysfunctional. As I get older, and have a family of my own, you realize no family is perfect. That's the genesis for the second installment of Antique Assassin, *Stranger Danger.*

I didn't know where the novel would go. But, almost every character in the story has family issues. Don't we all? Yet we don't choose our families and have to deal. There's still hope for loyalty, grace, and love despite our failures. Maybe that came through amidst the mayhem, killing, chaos... maybe not?

I wrote the first book in the series *Hired Gun* for NANOWRIMO (National Novel Writing Month). An international contest to write a first draft of a novel in 30 days (50,000 words).

I did it! December 2013, let it sit for over a year, had it edited, and published in June of 2015.

I loved the characters and the concept of the book. I needed to explore this world further. Hope you enjoyed it as much as I did writing it. I'm hoping to continue the series with a third book. And keep writing wherever my imagination takes me.

Stay connected, say hello, buy a book, all at ryanjpelton.com

Blessings,
Ryan J. Pelton
November 2016

# About the Author

Ryan J. Pelton is a genre-hopping author with over seventeen fiction and nonfiction titles to date. He also hosts a popular writing and publishing podcast (TheProlificWriter.net). Ryan reads, writes, and nurses a Diet Coke addiction, with his wife and four children in Kansas City, Missouri. Find Ryan and his work at: RyanJPelton.com.